PENGUIN BOOKS

SELECTED LETTERS

David Herbert Lawrence was born at Eastwood, Nottingham-shire, in 1885, fourth of the five children of a miner and his middle-class wife. He attended Nottingham High School and Nottingham University College. His first novel, *The White Peacock*, was published in 1911, just a few weeks after the death of his mother to whom he had been abnormally close. At this time he finally ended his relationship with Jessie Chambers (the Miriam of *Sons and Lovers*) and became engaged to Louie Burrows. His career as a schoolteacher was ended in 1911 by the illness which was ultimately diagnosed as tuberculosis.

In 1912 Lawrence eloped to Germany with Frieda Weekley, the German wife of his former modern languages tutor. They were married on their return to England in 1914. Lawrence was now living, precariously, by his writing. His greatest novels, *The Rainbow* and *Women in Love*, were completed in 1915 and 1916. The former was suppressed, and he could not find a publisher for the latter.

After the war Lawrence began his 'savage pilgrimage' in search of a more fulfilling mode of life than industrial Western civilization could offer. This took him to Sicily, Ceylon, Australia and, finally, New Mexico. The Lawrences returned to Europe in 1925. Lawrence's last novel, *Lady Chatterley's Lover*, was banned in 1928, and his paintings confiscated in 1929. He died in Vence in 1930 at the age of 44.

Lawrence spent most of his short life living. Nevertheless he produced an amazing quantity of work – novels, stories, poems, plays, essays, travel books, translations and letters . . . After his death Frieda wrote: 'What he had seen and felt and known he gave in his writing to his fellow men, the splendour of living, the hope of more and more life . . . a heroic and immeasurable gift.'

D. H. LAWRENCE

Letters

SELECTED BY
RICHARD ALDINGTON
WITH AN INTRODUCTION BY
ALDOUS HUXLEY

PENGUIN BOOKS
IN ASSOCIATION WITH
WILLIAM HEINEMANN LTD

Penguin Books Ltd, Harmondsworth,
Middlesex, England
Penguin Books, 625 Madison Avenue,
New York, New York 10022, U.S.A.
Penguin Books Australia Ltd, Ringwood,
Victoria, Australia
Penguin Books Canada Limited, 2801 John Street, Markham,
Ontario, Canada L3R 1B4
Penguin Books (N.Z.) Ltd, 182–190 Wairau Road,
Auckland 10, New Zealand

–

This selection first published in Penguin Books in Great Britain 1950
Reprinted 1954, 1961, 1968, 1971, 1976, 1978

Letters of D. H. Lawrence first published in
the United States of America by The Viking Press 1932
The Collected Letters of D. H. Lawrence first published in
the United States of America by The Viking Press 1962
This selection first published in Penguin Books in
the United States of America 1978

–

–

Printed in the United States of America by
Kingsport Press, Inc., Kingsport, Tennessee
Set in Monotype Garamond

–

An annotated edition of the complete correspondence of
D. H. Lawrence will be published in several volumes by
Cambridge University Press.

INTRODUCTION

'I ALWAYS say, my motto is "Art for my sake".' The words are from a letter written by Lawrence before the war. 'If I *want* to write, I write – and if I don't want to, I won't. The difficulty is to find exactly the form one's passion – work is produced by passion with me, like kisses – is it with you? – wants to take.'

'Art for my sake.' But even though for my sake, still art. Lawrence was always and unescapably an artist. Yes, unescapably is the word; for there were moment when he wanted to escape from his destiny. 'I wish from the bottom of my heart that the fates had not stigmatized me "writer". It is a sickening business.' But against the decree of fate there is no appeal. Nor was it by any means all the time that Lawrence wanted to appeal. His complaints were only occasional, and he was provoked to make them, not by any hatred of art as such, but by hatred of the pains and humiliations incidental to practising as an artist. Writing to Edward Garnett, 'Why, why,' he asks, 'should we be plagued with literature and such-like tomfoolery? Why can't we live decent, honourable lives, without the critics in the Little Theatre fretting us?' The publication of a work of art is always the exposure of a nakedness, the throwing of something delicate and sensitive to the 'asses, apes and dogs.' Mostly, however, Lawrence loved his destiny, loved the art of which he was a master – as who, that is a master, can fail to do? Besides, art, as he practised it, and as, at the bottom, every artist, even the most pharisaically 'pure', practises it, was 'art for my sake'. It was useful to him, pragmatically helpful. 'One sheds one's sicknesses in books – repeats and presents again one's emotions to be master of them.' And, anyhow, liking or disliking were finally irrelevant in the face of the fact that Lawrence was in a real sense possessed by his creative genius. He could not help himself. 'I am doing a novel,' he writes in an early letter, 'a novel which I have never grasped. Damn its eyes, there I am at p. 145 and

I've no notion what it's about. I hate it. F. says it is good. But it's like a novel in a foreign language I don't know very well – I can only just make out what it's about.' To this strange force within him, to this power that created his works of art, there was nothing to do but submit. Lawrence submitted, completely and with reverence. 'I often think one ought to be able to pray before one works – and then leave it to the Lord. Isn't it hard work to come to real grips with one's imagination – throw everything overboard. I always feel as though I stood naked for the fire of Almighty God to go through me – and it's rather an awful feeling. One has to be so terribly religious to be an artist.' Conversely, he might have added, one has to be terribly an artist, terribly conscious of 'inspiration' and the compelling force of genius, to be religious as Lawrence was religious.

It is impossible to write about Lawrence except as an artist. He was an artist first of all, and the fact of his being an artist explains a life which seems, if you forget it, inexplicably strange. In *Son of Woman*, Mr Middleton Murry has written at great length about Lawrence – but about a Lawrence whom you would never suspect, from reading that curious essay in destructive hagiography, of being an artist. For Mr Murry almost completely ignores the fact that his subject – his victim, I had almost said – was one whom 'the fates had stigmatized "writer".' His book is *Hamlet* without the Prince of Denmark – for all its metaphysical subtleties and its Freudian ingenuities, very largely irrelevant. The absurdity of his critical method becomes the more manifest when we reflect that nobody would ever have heard of a Lawrence who was not an artist.

An artist is the sort of artist he is, because he happens to possess certain gifts. And he leads the sort of life he does in fact lead, because he is an artist, and an artist with a particular kind of mental endowment. Now there are general abilities and there are special talents. A man who is born with a great share of some special talent is probably less deeply affected by nurture than one whose ability is generalized. His gift is his fate, and he follows a predestined course, from which no

6

ordinary power can deflect him. In spite of Helvetius and Dr Watson, it seems pretty obvious that no amount of education – including under that term everything from the Oedipus complex to the English Public School system – could have prevented Mozart from being a musician, or musicianship from being the central fact in Mozart's life. And how would a different education have modified the expression of, say, Blake's gift? It is, of course, impossible to answer. One can only express the unverifiable conviction that an art so profoundly individual and original, so manifestly 'inspired', would have remained fundamentally the same whatever (within reasonable limits) had been the circumstances of Blake's upbringing. Lawrence, as Mr F. R. Leavis insists, has many affinities with Blake. 'He had the same gift of knowing what he was interested in, the same power of distinguishing his own feelings and emotions from conventional sentiment, the same "terrifying honesty".' Like Blake, like any man possessed of great special talents, he was predestined by his gifts. Explanations of him in terms of a Freudian hypothesis of nurture may be interesting, but they do not explain. That Lawrence was profoundly affected by his love for his mother and by her excessive love for him, is obvious to anyone who has read *Sons and Lovers*. None the less it is, to me at any rate, almost equally obvious that even if his mother had died when he was a child, Lawrence would still have been, essentially and fundamentally, Lawrence. Lawrence's biography does not account for Lawrence's achievement. On the contrary, his achievement, or rather the gift that made the achievement possible, accounts for a great deal of his biography. He lived as he lived, because he was, intrinsically and from birth, what he was. If we would write intelligibly of Lawrence, we must answer, with all their implications, two questions: first, what sort of gifts did he have? and secondly, how did the possession of these gifts affect the way he responded to experience?

Lawrence's special and characteristic gift was an extraordinary sensitiveness to what Wordsworth called 'unknown modes of being'. He was always intensely aware of the mystery of the world, and the mystery was always for him a *numen*,

7

divine. Lawrence could never forget, as most of us almost continuously forget, the dark presence of the otherness that lies beyond the boundaries of man's conscious mind. This special sensibility was accompanied by a prodigious power of rendering the immediately experienced otherness in terms of literary art.

Such was Lawrence's peculiar gift. His possession of it accounts for many things. It accounts, to begin with, for his attitude towards sex. His particular experiences as a son and as a lover may have intensified his preoccupation with the subject; but they certainly did not make it. Whatever his experiences, Lawrence *must* have been preoccupied with sex; his gift made it inevitable. For Lawrence, the significance of the sexual experience was this: that, in it, the immediate, non-mental knowledge of divine otherness is brought, so to speak, to a focus – a focus of darkness. Parodying Matthew Arnold's famous formula, we may say that sex is something not ourselves that makes for – not righteousness, for the essence of religion is not righteousness; there is a spiritual world, as Kierkegaard insists, beyond the ethical – rather, that makes for life, for divineness, for union with the mystery. Paradoxically, this something not ourselves is yet a something lodged within us; this quintessence of otherness is yet the quintessence of our proper being. 'And God the Father, the Inscrutable, the Unknowable, we know in the flesh, in Woman. She is the door for our in-going and our out-coming. In her we go back to the Father; but like the witnesses of the transfiguration, blind and unconscious.' Yes, blind and unconscious; otherwise it is a revelation, not of divine otherness, but of very human evil. 'The embrace of love, which should bring darkness and oblivion, would with these lovers (the hero and heroine of one of Poe's tales) be a daytime thing, bringing more heightened consciousness, visions, spectrum-visions, prismatic. The evil thing that daytime love-making is, and all sex-palaver!' How Lawrence hated Eleonora and Ligeia and Roderick Usher and all such soulful Mrs Shandys, male as well as female! What a horror, too, he had of all Don Juans, all knowing sensualists and conscious libertines! (About the time he was writing *Lady*

Chatterley's Lover he read the memoirs of Casanova, and was profoundly shocked.) And how bitterly he loathed the Wilhelm-Meisterish view of love as an education, as a means to culture, a Sandow-exerciser for the soul! To *use* love in this way, consciously and deliberately, seemed to Lawrence wrong, almost a blasphemy. 'It seems to me queer,' he says to a fellow writer, 'that you prefer to present men chiefly – as if you cared for women not so much for what they were in themselves as for what the men saw in them. So that after all in your work women seem not to have an existence, save they are the projections of the men ... It's the *positivity* of women you seem to deny – make them sort of instrumental.' The instrumentality of Wilhelm Meister's women shocked Lawrence profoundly.

(Here, in a parenthesis, let me remark on the fact that Lawrence's doctrine is constantly invoked by people of whom Lawrence himself would passionately have disapproved, in defence of a behaviour which he would have found deplorable, or even revolting. That this should have happened is by no means, of course, a condemnation of the doctrine. The same philosophy of life may be good or bad according as the person who accepts it and lives by it is intrinsically fine or base. Tartuffe's doctrine was the same, after all, as Pascal's. There have been refined fetish-worshippers, and unspeakably swinish Christians. To the preacher of a new way of life the most depressing thing that can happen is, surely, success. For success permits him to see how those he has converted distort and debase and make ignoble parodies of his teaching. If Francis of Assisi had lived to be a hundred, what bitterness he would have tasted! Happily for the saint, he died at forty-five, still relatively undisillusioned, because still on the threshold of the great success of his order. Writers influence their readers, preachers their auditors – but always, at bottom, to be more themselves. If the reader's self happens to be intrinsically similar to the writer's, then the influence is what the writer would wish it to be. If he is intrinsically unlike the writer, then he will probably twist the writer's doctrine into a rationalization of beliefs, an excuse for behaviour, wholly alien to the beliefs and behaviour approved by the writer. Lawrence has

9

suffered the fate of every man whose works have exercised an influence upon his fellows. It was inevitable and in the nature of things.)

For someone with a gift for sensing the mystery of otherness, true love must necessarily be, in Lawrence's vocabulary, *nocturnal*. So must true knowledge. Nocturnal and tactual – a touching in the night. Man inhabits, for his own convenience, a home-made universe within the greater alien world of external matter and his own irrationality. Out of the illimitable blackness of that world the light of his customary thinking scoops, as it were, a little illuminated cave – a tunnel of brightness, in which, from the birth of consciousness to its death, he lives, moves, and has his being. For most of us this bright tunnel is the whole world. We ignore the outer darkness; or if we cannot ignore it, if it presses too insistently upon us, we disapprove, being afraid. Not so Lawrence. He had eyes that could see, beyond the walls of light, far into the darkness, sensitive fingers that kept him continually aware of the environing mystery. He could not be content with the home-made, human tunnel, could not conceive that anyone else should be content with it. Moreover – and in this he was unlike those others, to whom the world's mystery is continuously present, the great philosophers and men of science – he did not want to increase the illuminated area; he approved of the outer darkness, he felt at home in it. Most men live in a little puddle of light thrown by the gig-lamps of habit and their immediate interest; but there is also the pure and powerful illumination of the disinterested scientific intellect. To Lawrence, both lights were suspect, both seemed to falsify what was, for him, the immediately apprehended reality – the darkness of mystery. 'My great religion,' he was already saying in 1912, 'is a belief in the blood, the flesh, as being wiser than the intellect. We can go wrong in our minds. But what the blood feels, and believes, and says, is always true.' Like Blake, who had prayed to be delivered from 'single vision and Newton's sleep': like Keats, who had drunk destruction to Newton for having explained the rainbow, Lawrence disapproved of too much knowledge, on the score that it diminished men's sense of wonder and blunted their sensitiveness to the great mystery. His dislike of science was passionate and expressed itself in the most fantastically unreasonable terms. 'All scientists are liars,' he would say, when I brought up some experimentally established fact, which he happened to dislike. 'Liars, liars!' It was a most convenient theory. I remember in particular one long and violent argument on evolution, in the reality of which Lawrence always passionately disbelieved. 'But look at the evidence, Lawrence,' I insisted, 'look at all the evidence.' His answer was characteristic. 'But I don't care about evidence. Evidence doesn't mean anything to me. I don't feel it *here*.' And he pressed his two hands on his solar plexus. I abandoned the argument and thereafter never, if I could avoid it, mentioned the hated name of science in his presence. Lawrence could give so much, and what he gave was so valuable, that it was absurd and profitless to spend one's time with him disputing about a matter in which he absolutely refused to take a rational interest. Whatever the intellectual consequences, he remained through thick and thin unshakeably loyal to his own genius. The *daimon* which possessed him was, he felt, a divine thing, which he would never deny or explain away, never even ask to accept a compromise. This loyalty to his own self, or rather to his gift, to the strange and powerful *numen* which, he felt, used him as its tabernacle, is fundamental in Lawrence, and accounts, as nothing else can do, for all that the world found strange in his beliefs and his behaviour. It was not an incapacity to understand that made him reject those generalizations and abstractions by means of which the philosophers and the men of science try to open a path for the human spirit through the chaos of phenomena. Not incapacity, I repeat; for Lawrence had, over and above his peculiar gift, an extremely acute intelligence. He was a clever man as well as a man of genius. (In his boyhood and adolescence he had been a great passer of examinations.) He could have understood the aim and methods of science perfectly well if he had wanted to. Indeed, he did understand them perfectly well; and it was for that very reason that he rejected them. For the methods of science and critical philosophy were incompatible with the exercise of his gift – the immediate perception and artistic rendering of divine otherness. And their aim, which is to push back the frontier of the unknown, was not to be reconciled with his aim, which was to remain as intimately as possible in contact with the surrounding darkness. And so, in spite of their enormous prestige, he rejected science and critical philosophy; he remained loyal to his gift. Exclusively loyal. He would not attempt to qualify or explain his immediate knowledge of the mystery, would not even attempt to supplement it by other, abstract knowledge. 'These terrible, conscious birds, like Poe and his Ligeia, deny the very life that is in them; they want to turn it all into talk, into *knowing*. And so life, which will not be known, leaves them.' Lawrence refused to *know* abstractly. He preferred to live; and he wanted other people to live.

No man is by nature complete and universal; he cannot have first-hand knowledge of every kind of possible human experience. Universality, therefore, can be achieved only by those who mentally simulate living experience – by the knowers, in a word, by people like Goethe (an artist for whom Lawrence always felt the most intense repugnance).

Again, no man is by nature perfect, and none can spontaneously achieve perfection. The greatest gift is a limited gift. Perfection, whether ethical or aesthetic, must be the result of knowing and of the laborious application of knowledge. Formal aesthetics are an affair of rules and the best classical models; formal morality, of the ten commandments and the imitation of Christ.

Lawrence would have nothing to do with proceedings so 'unnatural', so disloyal to the gift, to the resident or visiting *numen*. Hence his aesthetic principle, that art must be wholly spontaneous, and, like the artist, imperfect, limited and transient. Hence, too, his ethical principle that a man's first moral duty is not to attempt to live above his human station, or beyond his inherited psychological income.

The great work of art and the monument more perennial than brass are, in their very perfection and everlastingness, inhuman – too much of a good thing. Lawrence did not approve of them. Art, he thought, should flower from an immediate impulse towards self-expression or communication, and should wither with the passing of the impulse. Of all building materials Lawrence liked adobe the best; its extreme plasticity and extreme impermanence endeared it to him. There could be no everlasting pyramids in adobe, no mathematically accurate Parthenons. Nor, thank heaven, in wood. Lawrence loved the Etruscans, among other reasons, because they built wooden temples, which have not survived. Stone oppressed him with its indestructible solidity, its capacity to take and indefinitely keep the hard uncompromising forms of pure geometry. Great buildings made him feel uncomfortable, even when they were beautiful. He felt something of the same discomfort in the presence of any highly finished work of art. In music, for example, he liked the folk-song, because it was a slight thing, born of immediate impulse. The symphony oppressed him; it was too big, too elaborate, too carefully and consciously worked out, too 'would-be' – to use a characteristic Lawrencian expression. He was quite determined that none of his writings should be 'would-be'. He allowed them to flower as they liked from the depths of his being and would never use his conscious intellect to force them into a semblance of more than human perfection, or more than human universality. It was characteristic of him that he hardly ever corrected or patched what he had written. I have often heard him say, indeed, that he was incapable of correcting. If he was dissatisfied with what he had written, he did not, as most authors do, file, clip, insert, transpose; he re-wrote. In other words, he gave the *daimon* another chance to say what it wanted to say. There are, I believe, three complete and totally distinct manuscripts of *Lady Chatterley's Lover*. Nor was this by any means the only novel that he wrote more than once. He was determined that all he produced should spring direct from the mysterious, irrational source of power within him. The conscious intellect should never be allowed to come and impose, after the event, its abstract pattern of perfection.

It was the same in the sphere of ethics as in that of art. 'They want me to have form: that means, they want me to have *their* pernicious, ossiferous, skin-and-grief form, and I won't.' This was written about his novels; but it is just as applicable to his life. Every man, Lawrence insisted, must be an artist in life, must create his own moral form. The art of living is harder than the art of writing. 'It is a much more delicate thing to make love, and win love, than to declare love.' All the more reason, therefore, for practising this art with the most refined and subtle sensibility; all the more reason for not accepting that 'pernicious skin-and-grief form' of morality, which *they* are always trying to impose on one. It is the business of the sensitive artist in life to accept his own nature as it is, not to try to force it into another shape. He must take the material given him – the weaknesses and irrationalities, as well as the sense and the virtues; the mysterious darkness and otherness no less than the light of reason and the conscious ego – must take them all and weave them together into a satisfactory pattern; *his* pattern, not somebody else's pattern. 'Once I said to myself: "How can I blame – why be angry?" . . . Now I say: "When anger comes with bright eyes, he may do his will. In me he will hardly shake off the hand of God. He is one of the archangels, with a fiery sword. God sent him – it is beyond my knowing".' This was written in 1910. Even at the very beginning of his career Lawrence was envisaging man as simply the locus of a polytheism. Given his particular gifts of sensitiveness and of expression it was inevitable. Just as it was inevitable that a man of Blake's peculiar genius should formulate the very similar doctrine of the independence of states of being. All the generally accepted systems of philosophy and of ethics aim at policing man's polytheism in the name of some Jehovah of intellectual and moral consistency. For Lawrence this was an indefensible proceeding. One god had as much right to exist as another, and the dark ones were as genuinely divine as the bright. Perhaps (since Lawrence was so specially sensitive to the quality of dark godhead and so specially gifted to express it in art), perhaps even more divine. Anyhow, the polytheism was a democracy. This conception of human nature resulted in the formulation of two rather surprising doctrines, one ontological and the other ethical. The first is what I may call the Doctrine of Cosmic Pointlessness. 'There is no point. Life and Love are life and love, a bunch of violets is a bunch of violets, and to drag in the idea of a point is to ruin everything. Live and let live, love and let love, flower and fade, and follow the natural curve, which flows on, pointless.'

Ontological pointlessness has its ethical counterpart in the doctrine of insouciance. 'They simply are eaten up with caring. They are so busy caring about Fascism or Leagues of Nations or whether France is right or whether Marriage is threatened, that they never know where they are. They certainly never live on the spot where they are. They inhabit abstract space, the desert void of politics, principles, right and wrong, and so forth. They are doomed to be abstract. Talking to them is like trying to have a human relationship with the letter x in algebra.' As early as 1911 his advice to his sister was: 'Don't meddle with religion. I would leave all that alone, if I were you, and try to occupy myself fully in the present.'

Reading such passages – and they abound in every book that Lawrence wrote – I am always reminded of that section of the *Pensées*, in which Pascal speaks of the absurd distractions with which men fill their leisure, so that there shall be no hole or cranny left for a serious thought to lodge itself in their consciousness. Lawrence also inveighs against *divertissements*, but not against the same *divertissements* as Pascal. For him, there were two great and criminal distractions. First, work, which he regarded as a mere stupefacient, like opium. ('Don't exhaust yourself too much,' he writes to an industrious friend; 'it is immoral.' Immoral, because, among other reasons, it is too easy, a shirking of man's first duty, which is to live. 'Think of the rest and peace, the positive sloth and luxury of idleness that work is.' Lawrence had a real puritan's disapproval of the vice of working. He attacked the gospel of work for the same reasons as Chrysippus attacked Aristotle's gospel of pure intellectualism – on the ground that it was, in the old Stoic's words, 'only a kind of amusement' and that real living was a more serious affair than labour or abstract speculations.) The other inexcusable distraction, in Lawrence's eyes, was 'spirituality', that lofty musing on the ultimate nature of things which constitutes, for Pascal, 'the whole dignity and business of man'. Pascal was horrified that human beings could so far forget the infinite and the eternal as to 'dance and play the lute and sing and make verses'. Lawrence was no less appalled that they could so far forget all the delights and difficulties of immediate living as to remember eternity and infinity, to say nothing of the League of Nations and the Sanctity of Marriage. Both were great artists; and so each is able to convince us that he is at any rate partly right. Just how far each is right, this is not the place to discuss. Nor, indeed, is the question susceptible of a definite answer. 'Mental consciousness,' wrote Lawrence, 'is a purely individual affair. Some men are born to be highly and delicately conscious.' Some are not. Moreover, each of the ages of man has its suitable philosophy of life. (Lawrence's, I should say, was not a very good philosophy for old age or failing powers.) Besides, there are certain conjunctions of circumstances in which spontaneous living is the great distraction and certain others in which it is almost criminal to divert oneself with eternity or the League of Nations. Lawrence's peculiar genius was such that he insisted on spontaneous living to the exclusion of ideals and fixed principles; on intuition to the exclusion of abstract reasoning. Pascal, with a very different gift, evolved, inevitably, a very different philosophy.

Lawrence's dislike of abstract knowledge and pure spirituality made him a kind of mystical materialist. Thus, the moon affects him strongly; therefore it cannot be a 'stony cold world, like a world of our own gone cold. Nonsense. It is a globe of dynamic substance, like radium or phosphorus, coagulated upon a vivid pole of energy.' Matter must be intrinsically as lively as the mind which perceives it and is moved by the perception. Vivid and violent spiritual effects must have correspondingly vivid and violent material causes. And, conversely, any violent feeling or desire in the mind must be capable of producing violent effects upon external matter. Lawrence could not bring himself to believe that the spirit can be moved, moved if need be to madness, without imparting the smallest corresponding movement to the external world. He was a subjectivist as well as a materialist; in other words, he believed in the possibility, in some form or another, of magic. Lawrence's mystical materialism found characteristic expression in the curious cosmology and physiology of his speculative essays, and in his restatement of the strange Christian doctrine of the resurrection of the body. To his mind, the survival of the spirit was not enough; for the spirit is a man's conscious identity, and Lawrence did not want to be always identical to himself; he wanted to know otherness – to know it by being it, know it in the living flesh, which is always essentially *other*. Therefore there must be a resurrection of the body.

Loyalty to his genius left him no choice; Lawrence had to insist on those mysterious forces of otherness which are scattered without, and darkly concentrated within, the body and mind of man. He had to, even though, by doing so, he imposed upon himself, as a writer of novels, a very serious handicap. For according to his view of things most of men's activities were more or less criminal distractions from the proper business of human living. He refused to write of such distractions; that is to say, he refused to write of the main activities of the contemporary world. But as though this drastic limitation of his subject were not sufficient, he went still further and, in some of his novels, refused to write even of human personalities in the accepted sense of the term. *The Rainbow* and *Women in Love* (and indeed to a lesser extent all his novels) are the practical applications of a theory which is set forth in a very interesting and important letter to Edward Garnett, dated June 5th, 1914. 'Somehow, that which is physic – non-human in humanity, is more interesting to me than the old-fashioned human element, which causes one to conceive a character in a certain moral scheme and make him consistent. The certain moral scheme is what I object to. In Turgenev, and in Tolstoi, and in Dostoievsky, the moral scheme into which all the characters fit – and it is nearly the same scheme – is, whatever the extraordinariness of the characters themselves, dull, old, dead. When Marinetti writes: "It is the solidity of a blade of steel that is interesting by itself, that is, the incomprehending and inhuman alliance of its molecules in resistance to, let us say, a bullet. The heat of a piece of wood or iron is in fact more passionate, for us, than the laughter or tears of a woman" – then I know what he means. He is stupid, as an artist, for contrasting the heat of the iron and the laugh of the woman. Because what is interesting in the laugh of the woman is the same as the binding of the molecules of steel or their action in heat: it is the inhuman will, call it physiology, or like Marinetti, physiology of matter, that fascinates me. I don't so much care about what the woman *feels* – in the ordinary usage of the word. That presumes an *ego* to feel with. I only care about what the woman *is* – what she is – inhumanly, physiologically, materially – according to the use of the word . . . You mustn't look in my novel for the old stable *ego* of the character. There is another *ego*, according to whose action the individual is unrecognizable, and passes through, as it were, allotropic states which it needs a deeper sense than any we've been used to exercise, to discover are states of the same single radically unchanged element. (Like as diamond and coal are the same pure single element of carbon. The ordinary novel would trace the history of the diamond – but I say, "Diamond, what! This is carbon." And my diamond might be coal or soot, and my theme is carbon.)'

The dangers and difficulties of this method are obvious. Criticizing Stendhal, Professor Saintsbury long since remarked on 'that psychological realism which is perhaps a more different thing from psychological reality than our clever ones for two generations have been willing to admit, or, perhaps, able to perceive'.

Psychological reality, like physical reality, is determined by our mental and bodily make-up. Common sense, working on the evidence supplied by our unaided senses, postulates a world in which physical reality consists of such things as solid tables and chairs, bits of coal, water, air. Carrying its investigations further, science discovers that these samples of physical reality are 'really' composed of atoms of different elements, and these atoms, in their turn, are 'really' composed of more or less numerous electrons and protons arranged in a variety of patterns. Similarly, there is a commonsense, pragmatic conception of psychological reality; and also an un-commonsense conception. For ordinary practical purposes we conceive human beings as creatures with characters. But analysis of their behaviour can be carried so far that they cease to have characters and reveal themselves as collections of psychological atoms. Lawrence (as might have been expected of a man who could always perceive the otherness behind the most reassuringly familiar phenomenon) took the un-commonsense view of psychology. Hence the strangeness of his novels; and hence also, it must be admitted, certain qualities of violent monotony and intense indistinctness, qualities which make some of them, for all their richness and their unexpected beauty, so curiously difficult to get through. Most of us are more interested in diamonds and coal than in undifferentiated carbon, however vividly described. I have known readers whose reaction to Lawrence's books was very much the same as Lawrence's own reactions to the theory of evolution. What he wrote meant nothing to them because they 'did not feel it *here*' – in the solar plexus. (That Lawrence, the hater of scientific knowing, should have applied to psychology methods which he himself compared to those of chemical analysis, may seem strange. But we must remember that his analysis was done, not intellectually, but by an immediate process of intuition; that he was able, as it were, to *feel* the carbon in diamonds and coal, to *taste* the hydrogen and oxygen in his glass of water.)

Lawrence, then, possessed, or, if you care to put it the other way round, was possessed by, a gift – a gift to which he was unshakeably loyal. I have tried to show how the possession and the loyalty influenced his thinking and writing. How did they affect his life? The answer shall be, as far as possible, in Lawrence's own words. To Catherine Carswell Lawrence once wrote: 'I think you are the only woman I have met who is so intrinsically detached, so essentially separate and isolated, as to be a real writer or artist or recorder. Your relations with other people are only excursions from yourself. And to want children, and common human fulfilments, is rather a falsity for you, I think. You were never made to "meet and mingle", but to

19

remain intact, *essentially*, whatever your experiences may be.'

Lawrence's knowledge of 'the artist' was manifestly personal knowledge. He knew by actual experience that 'the real writer' is an essentially separate being, who must not desire to meet and mingle and who betrays himself when he hankers too yearningly after common human fulfilments. All artists know these facts about their species, and many of them have recorded their knowledge. Recorded it, very often, with distress; being intrinsically detached is no joke. Lawrence certainly suffered his whole life from the essential solitude to which his gift condemned him. 'What ails me,' he wrote to the psychologist, Dr Trigant Burrow, 'is the absolute frustration of my primeval societal instinct . . . I think societal instinct much deeper than sex instinct – and societal repression much more devastating. There is no repression of the sexual individual comparable to the repression of the societal man in me, by the individual ego, my own and everybody else's . . . Myself, I suffer badly from being so cut off . . . At times one is *forced* to be essentially a hermit. I don't want to be. But anything else is either a personal tussle, or a money tussle; sickening: except, of course, just for ordinary acquaintance, which remains acquaintance. One has no real human relations – that is so devastating.' One has no real human relations: it is the complaint of every artist. The artist's first duty is to his genius, his *daimon*; he cannot serve two masters. Lawrence, as it happened, had an extraordinary gift for establishing an intimate relationship with almost anyone he met. 'Here' (in the Bournemouth boarding-house where he was staying after his illness, in 1912) 'I get mixed up in people's lives so – it's very interesting, sometimes a bit painful, often jolly. But I run to such close intimacy with folk, it is complicating. But I love to have myself in a bit of a tangle.' His love for his art was greater, however, than his love for a tangle; and, whenever the tangle threatened to compromise his activities as an artist, it was the tangle that was sacrificed: he retired. Lawrence's only deep and abiding human relationship was with his wife. ('It is hopeless for me,' he wrote to a fellow artist, 'to try to do anything without I have a woman at the back of me . . . Böcklin – or somebody like him – daren't sit in a café except with his back to the wall. I daren't sit in the world without a woman behind me ... A woman that I love sort of keeps me in direct communication with the unknown, in which otherwise I am a bit lost.') For the rest, he was condemned by his gift to an essential separateness. Often, it is true, he blamed the world for his exile. 'And it comes to this, that the *oneness* of mankind is destroyed in me (by the war). I am I, and you are you, and all heaven and hell lie in the chasm between. Believe me, I am infinitely hurt by being thus torn off from the body of mankind, but so it is and it is right.' It was right because, in reality, it was not the war that had torn him from the body of mankind; it was his own talent, the strange divinity to which he owed his primary allegiance. 'I will not live any more in this time,' he wrote on another occasion. 'I know what it is. I reject it. As far as I possibly can, I will stand outside this time. I will live my life and, if possible, be happy. Though the whole world slides in horror down into the bottomless pit ... I believe that the highest virtue is to be happy, living in the greatest truth, not submitting to the falsehood of these personal times.' The adjective is profoundly significant. Of all the possible words of disparagement which might be applied to our uneasy age 'personal' is surely about the last that would occur to most of us. To Lawrence it was the first. His gift was a gift of feeling and rendering the unknown, the mysteriously other. To one possessed by such a gift, almost any age would have seemed unduly and dangerously personal. He had to reject and escape. But when he had escaped, he could not help deploring the absence of 'real human relationships'. Spasmodically, he tried to establish contact with the body of mankind. There were the recurrent projects for colonies in remote corners of the earth; they all fell through. There were his efforts to join existing political organizations; but somehow 'I seem to have lost touch altogether with the "Progressive" clique. In Croydon, the Socialists are so stupid and the Fabians so flat.' (Not only in Croydon, alas.) Then, during the war, there was his plan to co-operate with a few friends to take independent political action; but 'I would like to be remote, in Italy, writing my suol's words. To have to speak in the body is a violation to me.' And in the end he wouldn't violate himself; he remained aloof, remote, 'essentially separate'. 'It isn't scenery one lives by,' he wrote from Cornwall in 1916, 'but the freedom of moving about alone.' How acutely he suffered from this freedom by which he lived! *Kangaroo* describes a later stage of the debate between the solitary artist and the man who wanted social responsibilities and contact with the body of mankind. Lawrence, like the hero of his novel, decided against contact. He was by nature not a leader of men, but a prophet, a voice crying in the wilderness – the wilderness of his own isolation. The desert was his place, and yet he felt himself an exile in it. To Rolf Gardiner he wrote, in 1926: 'I should love to be connected with something, with some few people, in something. As far as anything *matters*, I have always been very much alone, and regretted it. But I can't belong to clubs, or societies, or Freemasons, or any other damn thing. So if there is, with you, an activity I *can* belong to, I shall thank my stars. But, of course, I shall be wary beyond words, of committing myself.' He was in fact so wary that he never committed himself, but died remote and unconnected as he had lived. The *daimon* would not allow it to be otherwise.

(Whether Lawrence might not have been happier if he had disobeyed his *daimon* and forced himself at least into mechanical and external connexion with the body of mankind, I forbear to speculate. Spontaneity is not the only and infallible secret of happiness; nor is a 'would-be' existence necessarily disastrous. But this is by the way.)

It was, I think, the sense of being cut off that sent Lawrence on his restless wanderings round the earth. His travels were at once a flight and a search: a search for some society with which he could establish contact, for a world where the times were not personal, and conscious knowing had not yet perverted living; a search and at the same time a flight from the miseries and evils of the society into which he had been born, and for which, in spite of his artist's detachment, he could not help feeling profoundly responsible. He felt himself 'English in the teeth of all the world, even in the teeth of England': that was why he had to go to Ceylon and Australia and Mexico. He could not have felt so intensely English in England without involving himself in corporative political action, without belonging and being attached; but to attach himself was something he could not bring himself to do, something that the artist in him felt as a violation. He was at once too English and too intensely an artist to stay at home. 'Perhaps it is necessary for me to try these places, perhaps it is my destiny to know the world. It only excites the outside of me. The inside it leaves more isolated and stoic than ever. That's how it is. It is all a form of running away from oneself and the great problems, all this wild west and the strange Australia. But I try to keep quite clear. One forms not the faintest inward attachment, especially here in America.'

His search was as fruitless as his flight was ineffective. He could not escape either from his homesickness or his sense of responsibility; and he never found a society to which he could belong. In a kind of despair, he plunged yet deeper into the surrounding mystery, into the dark night of that otherness whose essence and symbol is the sexual experience. In *Lady Chatterley's Lover* Lawrence wrote the epilogue to his travels and, from his long and fruitless experience of flight and search, drew what was, for him, the inevitable moral. It is a strange and beautiful book; but inexpressibly sad. But then so, at bottom, was its author's life.

Lawrence's psychological isolation resulted, as we have seen, in his seeking physical isolation from the body of mankind. This physical isolation reacted upon his thoughts. 'Don't mind if I am impertinent,' he wrote to one of his correspondents at the end of a rather dogmatic letter. 'Living here alone one gets so different – sort of *ex cathedra*.' To live in isolation, above the medley, has its advantages; but it also imposes certain penalties. Those who take a bird's-eye view of the world often see clearly and comprehensively; but they tend to ignore all tiresome details, all the difficulties of social life and, ignoring, to judge too sweepingly and to condemn too lightly. Nietzsche spent his most fruitful years perched on the tops of mountains, or plunged in the yet more abysmal solitude of boarding-houses by the Mediterranean. That was why, a delicate and sensitive man, he could be so bloodthirstily censorious – so wrong, for all his gifts, as well as so right. From the deserts of New Mexico, from rustic Tuscany or Sicily, from the Australian bush, Lawrence observed and judged and advised the distant world of men. The judgements, as might be expected, were often sweeping and violent; the advice, though admirable so far as it went, inadequate. Political advice from even the most greatly gifted of religious innovators is always inadequate; for it is never, at bottom, advice about politics, but always about something else. Differences in quantity, if sufficiently great, produce differences of quality. This sheet of paper, for example, is qualitatively different from the electrons of which it is composed. An analogous difference divides the politician's world from the world of the artist, or the moralist, or the religious teacher. 'It is the business of the artist,' writes Lawrence, 'to follow it [the war] to the heart of the individual fighters – not to talk in armies and nations and numbers – but to track it home – home – their war – and it's at the bottom of almost every Englishman's heart – the war – the desire of war – the *will* to war – and at the bottom of every German heart.' But an appeal to the individual heart can have very little effect on politics, which is a science of averages. An actuary can tell you how many people are likely to commit suicide next year; and no artist or moralist or Messiah can, by an appeal to the individual heart, prevent his forecast from being remarkably correct. If the things which are Caesar's differ from the things which are God's, it is because Caesar's things are numbered by the thousands and millions, whereas God's things are single individual souls. The things of Lawrence's Dark God were not even individual souls; they were the psychological atoms whose patterned coming together constitutes a soul. When Lawrence offers political advice, it refers to matters which are not really political at all. The political world of enormous numbers was to him a nightmare, and he fled from it. Primitive communities are so small that their politics are essentially unpolitical; that, for Lawrence, was one of their greatest charms. Looking back from some far-away and underpopulated vantage point at the enormous, innumerable modern world, he was appalled by what he saw. He condemned, he advised, but at bottom and finally he felt himself impotent to deal with Caesar's alien and inhuman problems. 'I wish there were miracles,' was his final despairing comment. 'I am tired of the old laborious way of working things to their conclusions.' But, alas, there are no miracles, and faith, even the faith of a man of genius, moves no mountains.

Enough of explanation and interpretation. To those who knew Lawrence, not *why*, but *that* he was what he happened to be, is the important fact. I remember very clearly my first meeting with him. The place was London, the time 1915. But Lawrence's passionate talk was of the geographically remote and of the personally very near. Of the horrors in the middle distance – war, winter, the town – he would not speak. For he was on the point, so he imagined, of setting off to Florida – to Florida, where he was going to plant that colony of escape, of which up to the last he never ceased to dream. Sometimes the name and site of this seed of a happier and different world were purely fanciful. It was called Rananim, for example, and was an island like Prospero's. Sometimes it had its place on the map and its name was Florida, Cornwall, Sicily, Mexico and again, for a time, the English countryside. That wintry afternoon in 1915 it was Florida. Before tea was over he asked me if I would join the colony, and though I was an intellectually cautious young man, not at all inclined to enthusiasms, though Lawrence had startled and embarrassed me with sincerities of a kind to which my upbringing had not accustomed me, I answered yes.

Fortunately, no doubt, the Florida scheme fell through. Cities of God have always crumbled; and Lawrence's city – his village, rather, for he hated cities – his Village of the Dark God would doubtless have disintegrated like all the rest. It was better that it should have remained, as it was always to remain, a project and a hope. And I knew this even as I said I would join the colony. But there was something about Lawrence which made such knowledge, when one was in his presence, curiously irrelevant. He might propose impracticable schemes, he might say or write things that were demonstrably incorrect or even, on occasion (as when he talked about science), absurd. But to a very considerable extent it didn't matter. What mattered was always Lawrence himself, was the fire that burned within him, that glowed with so strange and marvellous a radiance in almost all he wrote.

My second meeting with Lawrence took place some years later, during one of his brief revisitings of that after-war England which he had come so much to dread and to dislike. Then in 1925, while in India, I received a letter from Spotorno. He had read some essays I had written on Italian travel; said he liked them; suggested a meeting. The next year we were in Florence and so was he. From that time, till his death, we were often together – at Florence, at Forte dei Marmi, for a whole winter at Diablerets, at Bandol, in Paris, at Chexbres, at Forte again, and finally at Vence where he died.

In a spasmodically kept diary I find this entry under the date of December 27th, 1927: 'Lunched and spent the p.m. with the Lawrences. D. H. L. in admirable form, talking wonderfully. He is one of the few people I feel real respect and admiration for. Of most other eminent people I have met I feel that at any rate I belong to the same species as they do. But this man has something different and superior in kind, not degree.'

'Different and superior in kind.' I think almost everyone who knew him well must have felt that Lawrence was this. A being, somehow, of another order, more sensitive, more highly conscious, more capable of feeling than even the most gifted of common men. He had, of course, his weaknesses and defects; he had his intellectual limitations – limitations which he seemed to have imposed deliberately upon himself. But these weaknesses and defects and limitations did not affect the fact of his superior otherness. They diminished him quantitively, so to speak; whereas the otherness was qualitative. Spill half your glass of wine and what remains is still wine. Water, however full the glass may be, is always tasteless and without colour.

To be with Lawrence was a kind of adventure, a voyage of

discovery into newness and otherness. For, being himself of a different order, he inhabited a universe different from that of common men – a brighter and intenser world, of which, while he spoke, he would make you free. He looked at things with the eyes, so it seemed, of a man who had been at the brink of death and to whom, as he emerges from the darkness, the world reveals itself as unfathomably beautiful and mysterious. For Lawrence, existence was one continuous convalescence; it was as though he were newly re-born from a mortal illness every day of his life. What these convalescent eyes saw his most casual speech would reveal. A walk with him in the country was a walk through that marvellously rich and significant landscape which is at once the background and the principal personage of all his novels. He seemed to know, by personal experience, what it was like to be a tree or a daisy or a breaking wave or even the mysterious moon itself. He could get inside the skin of an animal and tell you in the most convincing detail how it felt and how, dimly, inhumanly, it thought. Of Black-Eyed Susan, for example, the cow at his New Mexican ranch, he was never tired of speaking, nor was I ever tired of listening to his account of her character and her bovine philosophy.

'He sees,' Vernon Lee once said to me, 'more than a human being ought to see. Perhaps,' she added, 'that's why he hates humanity so much.' Why also he loved it so much. And not only humanity: nature too, and even the supernatural. For wherever he looked he saw more than a human being ought to see; saw more and therefore loved and hated more. To be with him was to find oneself transported to one of the frontiers of human consciousness. For an inhabitant of the safe metropolis of thought and feeling it was a most exciting experience.

One of the great charms of Lawrence as a companion was that he could never be bored and so could never be boring. He was able to absorb himself completely in what he was doing at the moment; and he regarded no task as too humble for him to undertake, nor so trivial that it was not worth his while to do it well. He could cook, he could sew, he could darn a stocking

27

and milk a cow, he was an efficient wood-cutter and a good hand at embroidery, fires always burned when he had laid them and a floor, after Lawrence had scrubbed it, was thoroughly clean. Moreover, he possessed what is, for a highly strung and highly intelligent man, an even more remarkable accomplishment: he knew how to do nothing. He could just sit and be perfectly content. And his contentment, while one remained in his company, was infectious.

As infectious as Lawrence's contented placidity were his high spirits and his laughter. Even in the last years of his life, when his illness had got the upper hand and was killing him inch-meal, Lawrence could still laugh, on occasion, with something of the old and exuberant gaiety. Often, alas, towards the end, the laughter was bitter, and the high spirits almost terrifyingly savage. I have heard him sometimes speak of men and their ways with a kind of demoniac mockery, to which it was painful, for all the extraordinary brilliance and profundity of what he said, to listen. The secret consciousness of his dissolution filled the last years of his life with an overpowering sadness. (How tragically the splendid curve of the letters droops, at the end, towards the darkness!) It was, however, in terms of anger that he chose to express this sadness. Emotional indecency always shocked him profoundly, and, since anger seemed to him less indecent as an emotion than a resigned or complaining melancholy, he preferred to be angry. He took his revenge on the fate that had made him sad by fiercely deriding everything. And because the sadness of the slowly dying man was so unspeakably deep, his mockery was frighteningly savage. The laughter of the earlier Lawrence and, on occasion, as I have said, even the later Lawrence was without bitterness and wholly delightful.

Vitality has the attractiveness of beauty, and in Lawrence there was a continuously springing fountain of vitality. It went on welling up to him, leaping, now and then, into a great explosion of bright foam and iridescence, long after the time when, by all the rules of medicine, he should have been dead. For the last two years he was like a flame burning on in miraculous disregard of the fact that there was no more fuel to justify its existence. One grew, in spite of constantly renewed alarms, so well accustomed to seeing the flame blazing away, self-fed, in its broken and empty lamp that one almost came to believe that the miracle would be prolonged, indefinitely. But it could not be. When, after several months of separation, I saw him again at Vence in the early spring of 1930, the miracle was at an end, the flame guttering to extinction. A few days later it was quenched.

Beautiful and absorbingly interesting in themselves, the letters which follow are also of the highest importance as biographical documents. In them, Lawrence has written his life and painted his own portrait. Few men have given more of themselves in their letters. Lawrence is there almost in his entirety. *Almost;* for he obeyed both of Robert Burns's injunctions:

> 'Aye free, aff han' your story tell,
> When wi' a bosom crony;
> But still keep something to yoursel'
> Ye scarcely tell to ony.'

The letters show us Lawrence as he was in his daily living. We see him in all his moods. (And it is curious and amusing to note how his mood will change according to his correspondent. 'My kindliness makes me sometimes a bit false,' he says of himself severely. In other words, he knew how to adapt himself. To one correspondent he is gay, at moments even larky – because larkiness is expected of him. To another he is gravely reflective. To a third he speaks the language of prophesying and revelation.) We follow him from one vividly seen and recorded landscape to another. We watch him during the war, a subjectivist and a solitary artist, desperately fighting his battle against the nightmare of objective facts and all the inhumanly numerous things that are Caesar's. Fighting and, inevitably, losing. And after the war we accompany him round the world, as he seeks, now in one continent now in another, some external desert to match the inner wilderness from which he utters his prophetic cry, or some community of which he can feel himself a member. We see him being drawn towards his fellows and then repelled again, making up his mind to force himself into some relation with society and then, suddenly, changing it again, and letting himself drift once more on the current of circumstances and his own inclinations. And finally, as his illness begins to get the better of him, we see him obscured by a dark cloud of sadness – the terrible sadness, out of which, in one mood, he wrote his savage *Nettles*, in another *The Man Who Died*, that lovely and profoundly moving story of the miracle for which somewhere in his mind he still hoped – still hoped, against the certain knowledge that it could never happen.

In the earlier part of his career especially, and again towards the end, Lawrence was a most prolific correspondent. There was, however, an intermediate period during his time of wandering, when he seems to have written very little. Of letters with the date of these after-war years, not more than a dozen or two have so far turned up; and there seems to be no reason to believe that further inquiries will reveal the existence of many more. It is not because they have been destroyed or are being withheld that Lawrence's letters of this period are so scarce; it is because, for one reason or another, he did not then care to write letters, that he did not want to feel himself in relationship with anyone. After a time, the stream begins again. But the later letters, though plentiful and good, are neither so numerous nor so richly and variously delightful as the earlier. One feels that Lawrence no longer wanted to give of himself so fully to his correspondents as in the past.

In selecting the letters which Lawrence's correspondents have so generously placed at my disposal, I have been guided by a few simple and obvious principles. Trivial notes have not been reproduced. Nor, in most cases, business letters. (There is, for example, an enormous correspondence referring to the publication and distribution of the first, Florentine edition of *Lady Chatterley*. This has been omitted altogether.) A certain number of passages that might have given pain to the person mentioned in them, or that deal with personalities which it did not seem right or decent to make public, have been cut out. Here and there, for obvious reason, I have suppressed a name.

In conclusion, I would like to express my thanks to Mrs Enid Hilton for her invaluable help in preparing this volume for the press. Lacking her co-operation, I should have been lost.

ALDOUS HUXLEY

1910

. . . Heinemann was very nice; doesn't want me to alter anything; will publish in Sept. or Oct., the best season; we have
signed agreements concerning royalties, and I have agreed to
give him the next novel. Will he want it? This transacting of
literary business makes me sick. I have no faith in myself at
the end, and I simply loathe writing. You do not know how
repugnant to me was the sight of that *Nethermere* MSS.* By
the way, I have got to find a new title. I wish, <u>from the bottom
of my heart, the fates had not stigmatized me 'writer'</u>. It is a
sickening business. Will you tell me whether the Saga is good?
I am rapidly losing faith in it . . .

I assure you I am not weeping into my register. It is only
that the literary world seems a particularly hateful yet powerful one. The literary element, like a disagreeable substratum
under a fair country, spreads under every inch of life, sticking
to the roots of the growing things. Ugh, that is hateful! I wish
I might be delivered . . .

2 TO EDWARD GARNETT

16, *Colworth Rd,*
Addiscombe, Croydon.
17 *Dec.,* 1911

DEAR GARNETT, –
I got the cheque yesterday, and accept it gladly from you.
But a little later, when I have some money, you must let me
pay it back to you, because that seems to me honester.
I am very well. Yesterday I sat up to tea for an hour. It is a

---

Nethermere was the early title of *The White Peacock:* the Saga was
issued as *The Trespasser.*

weird, not delightful experience, which makes me feel like the seated statues of kings in Egypt. My chest gets rapidly well, but my brain is too active. To keep myself at all in order, I ought to be up and doing. By nature I am ceaselessly active. Now I sleep badly, because I don't do enough – and I mustn't work, because then away goes my strength. But I feel my life burn like a free flame floating on oil – wavering and leaping and snapping. I shall be glad to get it confined and conducted again.

The doctor says I mustn't go to school again or I shall be consumptive. But he doesn't know. I shan't send in my notice, but shall ask for long leave of absence. Then I can go back if I get broke. The head-master grieves loudly over my prolonged absence. He knows he would scarcely get another man to do for him as I have done.

I shall look for you on Wednesday. Don't bring back that novel MSS. unless you have read all you want to read. I don't want it a bit. It is a work too chargé, too emotional. It's a sponge dipped too full of vinegar, or wine, or whatever – it wants squeezing out. I shrink from it rather. I wonder whether Jefferies used to wince away from the *Story of my Heart*.

This is too long a letter to send to a busy man: excuse me.

Yours sincerely,
D. H. LAWRENCE

3   TO EDWARD GARNETT

16, *Colworth Rd,*
Addiscombe, Croydon.
18 *Dec.,* 1911

DEAR GARNETT, –
Your letter concerning the Siegmund book is very exciting. I will tell you just what Hueffer said, then you will see the attitude his kind will take up.

'The book,' he said, 'is a rotten work of genius. It has no construction or form – it is execrably bad art, being all variations on a theme. Also it is erotic – not that I, personally, mind that, but an erotic work *must* be good art, which this is not.'

I sent it to our friend with the monocle. He wrote to me, after three months: 'I have read part of the book. I don't care for it, but we will publish it.'

I wrote back to him: 'No, I won't have the book published. Return it to me.'

That is about fifteen months ago. I wrote to Hueffer saying: 'The novel called *The Saga of Siegmund* I have determined not to publish.' He replied to me: 'You are quite right not to publish that book – it would damage your reputation perhaps permanently.'

When I was last up at Heinemann's, two months ago, I asked Atkinson to send me the MS. He promised to do so, and said: 'I have never finished it. It's your handwriting, you know', – a sweet smile. 'Perfectly legible, but so *tedious*' – a sweet smile.

That's all the criticism he ever ventured.

Is Hueffer's opinion worth anything, do you think? Is the book *so* erotic? I don't want to be talked about in an 'Ann Veronica' fashion.

If you offer the thing to Duckworth, do not, I beg you, ask for an advance on royalties. Do not present me as a beggar. Do not tell him I am poor. Heinemann owes me £50 in February – I have enough money to tide me over till he pays – and that fifty will, at home, last me six months. I do not want an advance – let me be presented to Duckworth as a respectable person.

Atkinson has not yet said anything about the poems. I told him I preferred only to publish about 25 of the best, impersonal pieces. He has not answered at all. I shall be glad when I have no more dealings with that firm.

You would get my yesterday's letter before you left the Cearne today – ?

We will, then, discuss the book on Wednesday. I shall change the title. Shall I call it *The Livanters* – is that a correct

35

noun from the verb 'To Livant'? To me, it doesn't look an ugly word, nor a disreputable one.

Yours sincerely,
D. H. LAWRENCE

4   TO EDWARD GARNETT

Compton House,
St Peter's Rd,
Bournemouth.
21 Jan., 1912

MY DEAR GARNETT, —

I received your letter yesterday, and the books this morning. It is very good of you, and it makes me wonder how you, who are as busy and as public a man as most literary fellows, can find the time and the energy. Hueffer impressed it on me, it couldn't be done: by the time a man was forty, the triviality of minor interests could only command a rare slight attention: and I had begun to believe it. But you are so prompt and consistently attentive, where you gain nothing, that I begin to reconsider myself.

I will send you herewith the 180 or 190 pages of the *Trespasser* which I have done. It won't take me much longer, will it? I hope the thing is knitted firm — I hate those pieces where the stitch is slack and loose. The *Stranger* piece is probably still too literary — I don't feel at all satisfied.

But this is a work one can't regard easily — I mean, at one's ease. It is so much oneself, one's naked self. I give myself away so much, and write what is my most palpitant, sensitive self, that I loathe the book, because it will betray me to a parcel of fools. Which is what any deeply personal or lyrical writer feels, I guess. I often think Stendhal must have writhed in torture every time he remembered *Le Rouge et le Noir* was public property: and Jefferies at *The Story of my Heart*. I don't like *The Story of my Heart*.

I wish the *Trespasser* were to be issued privately, to a few folk who had understanding. But I suppose by all the rules of life, it must take open chance, if it's good enough.

I like the first two stories of Gertrude Bone immensely – she is wonderfully perceptive there. She's got a lot of poetic feeling, a lot of perceptivity, but she seems scarcely able to concentrate it on her people she is studying: at least, not always. Something in Andreyev makes him rather uninteresting to me, and *House of Cobwebs* is, as Seacombe suggests, chiefly of interest as footnotes on Gissing. Gissing hasn't enough energy, enough sanguinity, to capture me. But I esteem him a good deal.

I am pretty well – have had a damnable cold, which lingers. The weather here is soft and inclined to fog. I would rather be braced a little, now.

I shall leave here on Feb. 3rd and will come straight to the Cearne, if that is convenient. I have promised to go home to Nottingham on Feb. 8th. Can you keep me at the Cearne about four days?

Here I get mixed up in people's lives so – it's very interesting, sometimes a bit painful, often jolly. But I run to such close intimacy with folk, it is complicating. But I love to have myself in a bit of a tangle.

Thanks very much for the things.

Yours,

D. H. LAWRENCE

5   TO EDWARD GARNETT

Queen's Square,
Eastwood, Notts.
17 *April,* 1912

DEAR GARNETT,–

Did I answer your last letter? I can't for my life remember. Why do you take so much trouble for me? – if I am not eternally grateful, I am a swine.

It is huge to think of Iden Payne acting me on the stage: you are like a genius of *Arabian Nights*, to get me through. Of course I will alter and improve whatever I can, and Mr Payne has fullest liberty to do entirely as he pleases with the play – you know that. And of course I don't expect to get money by it. But it's ripping to think of my being acted.

I shall be in London next week, I think – from Thursday to Sunday – then I can see Walter de la Mare, and Harrison, who want to jaw me, and you who don't want to jaw me. Mrs — will be in town also. She is ripping – she's the finest woman I've ever met – you must above all things meet her . . . she is the daughter of Baron von Richthofen, of the ancient and famous house of Richthofen – but she's splendid, she is really. How damnably I mix things up. Mrs — is perfectly unconventional, but really good – in the best sense. I'll bet you've never met anybody like her, by a long chalk. You *must* see her next week. I wonder if she'd come to the Cearne, if you asked us. Oh, but she is the woman of a lifetime.

I shall love to see you again. Don't be grumpy.

Yours,
D. H. LAWRENCE

6   To EDWARD GARNETT

Hotel Rheinischer Hof,
Trier.

9 *May*, 1912

DEAR GARNETT,–

I've not had any letters since I've been here – since Friday, that is – so I don't know what is taking place. Write to me, I beg you – I am staying in Trier till next Monday or Tuesday – then, for a week or two, my address will be c/o Frau Karl Krenkow, Waldröl, Rheinprovinz.

Of course I've been in Metz with Mrs —'s people. There's such a hell of a stir up. Nothing is settled yet. — knows everything. Oh Lord, what a mess to be in – and this after eight weeks of acquaintance! But I don't care a damn what it all costs. I'll tell you how things work out. At present all is vague.

I had to quit Metz because the damn fools wanted to arrest me as a spy. Mrs — and I were lying on the grass near some water – talking – and I was moving round an old emerald ring on her finger, when we heard a faint murmur in the rear – a German policeman. There was such a to-do. It needed all the fiery little Baron von Richthofen's influence – and he *is* rather influential in Metz – to rescue me. They vow I am an English officer – *I – I!!* The damn fools. So behold me, fleeing eighty miles away, to Trier. Mrs — is coming on Saturday. Oh Lord, it's easier to write history than to make it, even in such a mild way as mine.

Tell me if my literary affairs are shifting at all. Regards to Miss Whale.

Yours,
D. H. LAWRENCE

Isn't it all funny!

7   TO MRS S. A. HOPKIN

bei Professor Alf. Weber,
Icking,
bei München.

2 *June*, 1912

DEAR MRS HOPKIN,–
Although I haven't heard from you, I'll get a letter off to you, because to people I like, I always want to tell my good news. When I came to Germany I came with Mrs — went to Metz with her. Her husband knows all about it – but I don't think he will give her a divorce – only a separation. I wish he'd divorce her, so we could be married. But that's as it is.

I came down from the Rhineland to Munich last Friday week. Frieda met me there, in Munich. She had been living with her sister in a village down the Isar Valley, next village to this. We stayed in Munich a night, then went down to Beuerberg for eight days. Beuerberg is about 40 kilometres from Munich, up the Isar, near the Alps. This is the Bavarian Tyrol. We stayed in the Gasthaus zur Post. In the morning we used to have breakfast under the thick horse-chestnut trees, and the red and white flowers fell on us. The garden was on a ledge, high over the river, above the weir, where the timber rafts floated down. The Loisach – that's the river – is pale jade green, because it comes from glaciers. It is fearfully cold and swift. The people were all such queer Bavarians. Across from the inn, across a square full of horse-chestnut trees, was the church and the convent, so peaceful, all whitewashed, except for the minaret of the church, which has a black hat. Every day, we went out for a long, long time. There are flowers so many they would make you cry for joy – Alpine flowers. By the river, great hosts of globe flowers, that we call bachelor's buttons – pale gold great bubbles – then primulas, like mauve cowslips, somewhat – and queer marsh violets, and orchids, and lots of bell-flowers, like large, tangled, dark-purple hare-bells, and stuff like larkspur, very rich, and lucerne, so pink, and in the woods, lilies of the valley – oh, flowers, great wild mad profusion of them, everywhere. One day we went to a queer old play done by the peasants – this is the Ober-Ammergau country. One day we went into the mountains, and sat, putting Frieda's rings on our toes, holding our feet under the pale green water of a lake, to see how they looked. Then we go to Wolfratshausen where Frieda's sister has a house – like a chalet – on the hill above the white village.

Now Frieda and I are living alone in Professor Weber's flat. It is the top storey of this villa – quite small – four rooms beside kitchen. But there's a balcony, where we sit out, and have meals, and I write. Down below, is the road where the bullock wagons go slowly. Across the road the peasant women work in the wheat. Then the pale, milk-green river runs between the woods and the plain – then beyond, the mountains, range beyond range, and their tops glittering with snow.

I've just had to run into the kitchen – a jolly little place –

wondering what Frieda was up to. She'd only banged her head on the cupboard. So we stood and looked out. Over the hills was a great lid of black cloud, and the mountains nearest went up and down in a solid blue-black. Through, was a wonderful gold space, with a tangle of pale, wonderful mountains, peaks pale gold with snow, and farther and farther away – such a silent, glowing confusion, brilliant with snow. Now the thunder is going at it, and the rain is here.

I love Frieda so much, I don't like to talk about it. I never knew what love was before. She wanted me to write to you. I want you and her to be friends always. Sometimes perhaps she – perhaps we – shall need you. Then you'll be good to us, won't you?

The world is wonderful and beautiful and good beyond one's wildest imagination. Never, never, never could one conceive what love is, beforehand, never. Life can be great – quite god-like. It can be so. God be thanked I have proved it.

You might write to us here. Our week of honeymoon is over. Lord, it was lovely. But this – do I like this better? – I like it so much. Don't tell anybody. This is only for the good to know. Write to us.

D. H. LAWRENCE

8   TO MRS S. A. HOPKIN

Mayrhofen 138, *in Zillertal,*
Tirol, Austria.
19 *Aug.,* 1912

You know that it is not forgetfulness makes us not write to you. You know you are one of the very, very few who will take us into your heart, together. So, if the months go by without your hearing, I know you will understand – I know you will be sticking by us, and we shall be depending on you. I wanted my sister to come and talk with you, but she wouldn't; you see, it is harder for her, she is young, and doesn't understand quite. And she is going to marry Eddie Clarke in the spring, is going to become a hard, respectable married woman – I think the thought of me is very bitter to her – and she won't speak of me to anybody. Only she, of all my people, knows. And I told Jessie to leave her a chance of ridding herself of my influence: nobody else. Mrs — writes me – I told her I was with another woman – but no details. I am sorry for her, she is so ill.

Things have been hard, and worth it. There has been some sickening misery ... F. is to see the children, and stay with them, next Easter. It has been rather ghastly, that part of the affair. If only one didn't hurt so many people.

For ourselves, Frieda and I have struggled through some bad times into a wonderful naked intimacy, all kindled with warmth, that I know at last is love. I think I ought not to blame women, as I have done, but myself, for taking my love to the wrong woman, before now. Let every man find, keep on trying till he finds, the woman who can take him and whose love he can take, then who will grumble about men or about women. But the thing must be two-sided. At any rate, and whatever happens, I do love, and I am loved. I have given and I have taken – and that is eternal. Oh, if only people could marry properly; I believe in marriage.

Perhaps Frieda will have to come to London to see her husband, in the autumn. Then she might want you to help her. Would you go to London, if she needed you?

We think of spending the winter in Italy, somewhere on Lake Garda. We shall be awfully poor, but don't mind so long as we can manage. It is — and the children that are the trouble. You see he loves Frieda madly, and can't let go.

We walked from the Isarthal down here – or at least, quite a long way – F. and I – with our German shoulder-bags on our backs. We made tea and our meals by the rivers. Crossing the mountains, we got stranded one night. I found a lovely little wooden chapel, quite forsaken, and lit the candles, and looked at the hundreds of Ex Voto pictures – so strange. Then I found F. had gone. But she came back to the shrine, saying we were at the top of the pass and there was a hay-hut in the Alpine meadow. There we slept that night. In the dawn, the peaks were round us, and we were, as it seemed, in a pot, with a green high meadow for a bottom.

Here we are lodging awhile in a farmhouse. A mountain stream rushes by just outside. It is icy and clear. We go out all day with our rucksacks – make fires, boil eggs, and eat the lovely fresh gruyère cheese that they make here. We are almost pure vegetarians. We go quite long ways up the valleys. The peaks of the mountains are covered with eternal snow. Water comes falling from a fearful height, and the cows, in the summer meadows, tinkle their bells. Sometimes F. undresses and lies in the sun – sometimes we bathe together – and we *can* be happy, nobody knows how happy.

There are millions of different bells: tiny harebells, big, black-purple mountain harebells, pale blue, hairy, strange creatures, blue and white Canterbury bells – then there's a great blue gentian, and flowers like monkey-musk. The Alpine roses are just over – and I believe we could find the edelweiss if we tried. Sometimes we drink with the mountain peasants in the Gasthaus, and dance a little. And how we love each other – God only knows.

We shall be moving on soon, walking south, by the Brenner, to Italy. If you write, address us at 'Haus Vogelnest' – Wolfratshausen – bei München. F., with me, sends love.

Yours,
D. H. LAWRENCE

9   TO EDWARD GARNETT

Villa Leonardi, Riva,
Süd Tirol, Austria.
Monday (date between Sept. 7th
and Oct. 3rd, 1912)

DEAR GARNETT, –

Your letter came yesterday – of course we got yours and David's from Bozen. And this morning Duckworth sent me

£50 in notes – the angel! We are both bursting with joy and puffed up with importance. Also we've got a place to live in.

Frieda hates me because I daren't broach these Italians about flats and rooms. We know about 10 words of Italian. She hankered after a red place at Torbole. We hesitated for hours. Then she attacked a man, with three words.

'Prego – er – er – quartiere – d'affitare.' And he insists on our taking the 3.30 omnibus to Riva, so that at last we run in terror, seeing ourselves in that bus.

But we're going to Gargnano. The hotel lady sent us to Pietro di Paoli. We found him, a grey old Italian with grand manners and a jaw like a dog and a lovely wife of forty. Frieda adores Pietro and I the wife. They have to let, furnished, the bottom flat of the Villa Igéa – dining-room, kitchen, 2 bedrooms, furnished – big pretty rooms looking over the road on to the lake – a nice garden with peaches and bamboos – not big – for 80 lire a month: about 66/– a month – everything supplied, everything nice, nothing common – 3 windows in the dining-room – clean as a flower. And so, we are moving in on Wednesday, and you must come to see us quick, it's so nice.

Gargnano is a rather tumble-downish place on the lake. You can only get there by steamer, because of the steep rocky mountainy hills at the back – no railway. You would come via Brescia, I should think. There are vineyards and olive woods and lemon gardens on the hills at the back. There is a lovely little square, where the Italians gossip and the fishermen pull up their boats, just near. Everything is too nice for words – not a bit touristy – quite simply Italian common village – Riva is 20 or 25 kilometres, and Gardone 15. Come quick while the sun shines as it shines now, and the figs and peaches are ripe, and when the grape harvest begins. You can have the other bedroom. There will only be the three of us in the flat. You can go to Venice if you feel swanky. It won't cost you anything at the Villa Igéa, so there's only train fare. F. and I are hugging each other with joy at the idea of a *ménage*, and gorgeous copper pans in the kitchen, and steps down from the dining-room to the garden, and a view of the lake, which is

only 50 yards away. And you sound so jolly yourself. And if you want to send anybody for a holiday, they can come to us.
Love from both.

D. H. LAWRENCE

Address Villa Igéa, *Villa di Gargnano*, Lago di Garda, Italy. Pietro di Paoli writes and talks the most lovely French – quaintest thing on earth. I am hugely pleased about the *Love Poems and Others* – and I shall correct the proofs in Gargnano. What bliss. Only F. thinks they are trivial poems. She wants those concerning herself to blossom forth. – D. H. L.

10 TO A. W. McLEOD

Villa Igéa,
Villa di Gargnano,
Lago di Garda, Italy.
Friday, 6th October, 1912

DEAR MAC, –

Your books came today, your letter long ago. Now I am afraid I put you to a lot of trouble and expense, and feel quite guilty. But thanks a thousand times. And F. thanks you too.

I have read *Anna of the Five Towns* today, because it is stormy weather. For five months I have scarcely seen a word of English print, and to read it makes me feel fearfully queer. I don't know where I am. I am so used to the people going by outside, talking or singing some foreign language, always Italian now: but today, to be in Hanley, and to read almost my own dialect, makes me feel quite ill. I hate England and its hopelessness. I hate Bennett's resignation. Tragedy ought really to be a great kick at misery. But *Anna of the Five Towns* seems like an acceptance – so does all the modern stuff since Flaubert. I hate it. I want to wash again quickly, wash off England, the oldness and grubbiness and despair.

Today it is so stormy. The lake is dark, and with white

45

lambs all over it. The steamer rocks as she goes by. There are no sails stealing past. The vines are yellow and red, and fig trees are in flame on the mountains. I can't bear to be in England when I am in Italy. It makes me feel so soiled. Yesterday F. and I went down along the lake towards Maderno. We climbed down from a little olive wood, and swam. It was evening, so weird, and a great black cloud trailing over the lake. And tiny little lights of villages came out, so low down, right across the water. Then great lightnings split out. – No, I don't believe England need be so grubby. What does it matter if one is poor, and risks one's livelihood, and reputation. One *can* have the necessary things, life, and love, and clean warmth. Why is England so shabby?

The Italians here sing. They are very poor, they buy two-penn'orth of butter and a penn'orth of cheese. But they are healthy and they lounge about in the little square where the boats come up and nets are mended, like kings. And they go by the window proudly, and they don't hurry or fret. And the women walk straight and look calm. And the men adore children – they are glad of their children even if they're poor. I think they haven't many ideas, but they look well, and they have strong blood.

I go in a little place to drink wine near Bogliaco. It is the living-room of the house. The father, sturdy as these Italians are, gets up from table and bows to me. The family is having supper. He brings me red wine to another table, then sits down again, and the mother ladles him soup from the bowl. He has his shirt-sleeves rolled up and his shirt collar open. Then he nods and 'click-clicks' to the small baby, that the mother, young and proud, is feeding with soup from a big spoon. The grandfather, white-moustached, sits a bit effaced by the father. A little girl eats soup. The grandmother by the big, open fire sits and quietly scolds another little girl. It reminds me so of home when I was a boy. They are all so warm with life. The father reaches his thick brown hand to play with the baby – the mother looks quickly away, catching my eye. Then he gets up to wait on me, and thinks my bad Italian can't understand that a quarter litre of wine is 15 centesimi (1¼d.) when I give

46

him thirty. He doesn't understand tips. And the huge lot of figs for 20 centesimi.

Why can't you ever come? You could if you wanted to, at Christmas. Why not? We should love to have you, and it costs little. Why do you say I sark you about your letters? – I don't, they *are* delightful. I think I am going to Salo tomorrow and can get you some views of the lake there. I haven't got the proofs of my poems yet. It takes so long. Perhaps I will send you the MS. of *Paul Morel* – I shall alter the title – when it's done.

Thanks – *je te serre la main.*

D. H. LAWRENCE

11　　　　　　　　　To Edward Garnett

Villa Igéa, Villa di Gargnano,
(Brescia) Lago di Garda,
Italy.

14 *Nov.,* 1912

DEAR GARNETT, –
Your letter has just come. I hasten to tell you I sent the MS. of the *Paul Morel* novel to Duckworth registered, yesterday. And I want to defend it, quick. I wrote it again, pruning it and shaping it and filing it in. I tell you it has got form – *form:* haven't I made it patiently, out of sweat as well as blood. It follows this idea: a woman of character and refinement goes into the lower class, and has no satisfaction in her own life. She has had a passion for her husband, so the children are born of passion, and have heaps of vitality. But as her sons grow up she selects them as lovers – first the eldest, then the second. These sons are *urged* into life by their reciprocal love of their mother – urged on and on. But when they come to manhood, they can't love, because their mother is the strongest power in their lives, and holds them. It's rather like Goethe and his mother and Frau von Stein and Christiana – As soon as the

47

young men come into contact with women, there's a split. William gives his sex to a fribble, and his mother holds his soul. But the split kills him, because he doesn't know where he is. The next son gets a woman who fights for his soul – fights his mother. The son loves the mother – all the sons hate and are jealous of the father. The battle goes on between the mother and the girl, with the son as object. The mother gradually proves stronger, because of the tie of blood. The son decides to leave his soul in his mother's hands, and, like his elder brother, go for passion. He gets passion. Then the split begins to tell again. But, almost unconsciously, the mother realizes what is the matter, and begins to die. The son casts off his mistress, attends to his mother dying. He is left in the end naked of everything, with the drift towards death.

It is a great tragedy, and I tell you I have written a great book. It's the tragedy of thousands of young men in England – it may even be Bunny's tragedy. I think it was Ruskin's, and men like him. – Now tell me if I haven't worked out my theme, like life, but always my theme. Read my novel. It's a great novel. If *you* can't see the development – which is slow, like growth – I can.

As for the *Fight for Barbara* – I don't know much about plays. If ever you have time, you might tell me where you find fault with the *Fight for Barbara*. *The Merry Go Round* and the other are candidly impromptus. I *know* they want doing again – recasting. I should like to have them again, now, before I really set to work on my next novel – which I have conceived – and I should like to try re-casting and re-forming them. If you have time, send them me.

I should like to dedicate the *Paul Morel* to you – may I? But not unless you think it's really a good work. 'To Edward Garnett, in Gratitude.' But you can put it better.

You are miserable about your play. Somehow or other your work riles folk. Why does it? But it makes them furious. Nevertheless, I shall see the day when a volume of your plays is in all the libraries. I can't understand why the dreary weeklies haven't read your *Jeanne* and installed it as a 'historical document of great value'. You know they hate you as a creator, all the critics: but why they shouldn't sigh with relief at finding you – in their own conceptions – a wonderfully subtle renderer and commentator of history, I don't know.

Pinker wrote me the other day, wanting to place me a novel with one of the leading publishers. Would he be any good for other stuff? It costs so many stamps, I don't reply to all these people.

Have I made those naked scenes in *Paul Morel* tame enough? You cut them if you like. Yet they are so clean – and I *have* patiently and laboriously constructed that novel.

It is a marvellous moonlight night. The mountains have shoulder-capes of snow. I have been far away into the hills today, and got great handfuls of wild Christmas roses. This is one of the most beautiful countries in the world. You must come. The sunshine is marvellous, on the dark blue water, the ruddy mountains' feet, and the snow.

F. and I keep struggling forward. It is not easy, but I won't complain. I suppose, if in the end I can't make enough money by writing, I shall have to go back to teaching. At any rate I can do that, so matters are never hopeless with me.

When you have time, do tell me about the *Fight for Barbara*. You think it couldn't be any use for the stage? I think the new generation is rather different from the old. I think they will read me more gratefully. But there, one can only go on.

It's funny, there is no *war* here – except 'Tripoli'. Everybody sings Tripoli. The soldiers howl all the night through and bang tambourines when the wounded heroes come home. – And the Italian papers are full of Servia and Turkey – but what has England got to do with it?

It's awfully good of you to send me a paper. But you'll see, one day I can help you, or Bunny. And I will.

You sound so miserable. It's the damned work. I wish you were here for a while. If you get run down, do come quickly. *Don't* let yourself become ill. This is such a beastly dangerous time. And you could work here, and live cheap as dirt with us.

Don't mind if I am impertinent. Living here alone one gets so different – sort of *ex cathedra*.

D. H. LAWRENCE

Villa Igéa,
    Villa di Gargnano,
        Lago di Garda (Brescia).
            17 Jan., 1913

Dear Mac, –

It's high time I wrote and thanked you for the notes and book. It's a delightful little Burns. And Henley was awfully good, but made me rather wild. Frieda and I have had high times, arguing over Andrew Lang and Henley and Lockhart. As for the book, my novel on the subject, I wonder if I shall ever get it done. I have written 80 pages of a new novel: a most curious work, which gives me great joy to write, but which, I am afraid, will give most folk extreme annoyance to read, if it doesn't bore them.

We've got a theatre here, and last night I went to see *Amletto*. Do you recognize our old friend? Now he was, really, the most amazing creature you can imagine: rather short, rather stout, with not much neck, and about forty years old: a bit after the Caruso type of Italian: the Croton type. I almost fell out of my little box trying to suppress my laughter. Because being one of the chief persons in the audience, and of course, the only Englishman, and ranking here as quite a swell – they acted particularly for me. I sat in my box No. 8, and felt a bigger farce than the stage. Poor Amletto – when he came forward whispering – 'Essere – o non essere,' I thought my ears would fall off. When the gravedigger holds up a skull and says, 'Ecco, Signore! Questo cranio è quel – ' I almost protested. Hamlet addressed as Signore! – No – it was too much. I saw *Ghosts* and gulped it down – it was rather good. I have seen a D'Annunzio play, and rather enjoyed it – fearful melodrama. But they are only peasants, the players, and they play farces: the queen is always the old servant woman, born for the part; and the king is always the contadino, or the weedy, weedy, old father – also born for the part. And Hamlet is usually the villain in some 'amour' – and poor Amletto, if I hadn't known what it was all about, I should have thought he had murdered some madam '*à la* Crippen' and it was *her* father's ghost chasing him: whilst he dallied between a bad and murderous conscience, a slinking desire to avoid everybody, and a wicked hankering after 'Ofaylia' – that's what she sounds like. I am muddled.

It's nasty weather – a beastly wind from the Po that has brought the snow right down the mountains, not many yards above us. I object. I came here for sunshine, and insist on having it.

I got the blues thinking of the future, so I left off and made some marmalade. It's amazing how it cheers one up to shred oranges or scrub the floor.

Did H. H. send you the pictures all right? He's a lazy devil. If they've not come, drop him a p.c. and ask if he's posted them to the wrong address. Write me a letter soon: it is nice to feel one's folk in England. Tell F. T. I'll write him soon. My love to everybody.

D. H. LAWRENCE

13   To DAVID GARNETT

Villa Igéa,
Villa di Gargnano,
Lago di Garda (*Brescia*).
18 *Feb.*, 1913

MY DEAR BUNNY, –

It's a beastly shame we don't write to you. But you read your father's letters from us, don't you? And I'm sure they're enough, you won't want any more.

I am glad not to be coming to England just yet. It is funny how I dread my native land. But here it is so free. The tightness of England is horrid.

The spring is here – violets and primroses in profusion, and beautiful tufts of heather. F. and I went to Campione on Sunday – about 10 miles up the lake.

It's a queer place – just a flat strip of land at the foot of great cliffs, and mere cotton mills, and workmen's dwellings – all perfectly isolated, on a little ledge that the lake washes. Well, having got into Campione, we couldn't get out. I wanted to find a road, but Frieda rushed to the first man, and asked him. He turned out to be fearfully drunk, and said he would guide us over the gallery. We went a little way – the gallery is quite a fantastic path that climbs the gorge, under a great spurt of water. Well, I wanted to send him back, because we could go by ourselves, and being so drunk, he was winking at Frieda over my shoulder. She was terrified. He wouldn't think of returning. I had an altercation with him, and he threatened to throw me into the stream – all this on the steps of the gallery, like flies on the side of a wall. We retreated – he was furious. And the dialect they speak is quite unintelligble to me. At last I got some youths to hang on to him whilst we mounted the gallery. There were ropes of ice where the stream leaps over the path. Then one must go through tunnels, on boards laid over the stream, the water running just below one's feet, the rock about neck-high, and beastly dark. It took us an hour and a half, hard going, to climb out of Campione. Then we were among the snow, fearfully wild. And these deserted Italian villages stand so like rubble of rocks between the hills. The old maize stalks shook in an icy wind above a snow field that gleamed like silver. It is pretty.

In Gardola di Tignale – the next village – the brass band was playing for a major returned from Tripoli, and he was standing in his doorway while the band brayed in his honour on his doorstep. The landlord of the inn was an awfully jolly old sport. The inns are the living-room of the family – dogs, babies, boiling pots, villains, and great open chimneys in which one sits. The hearth is raised about 3 ft, so one sits in a high, high chair – a chair on stilts – with one's feet near the ashes, and drinks moscato – *Asti spumante* I think it's called – or muscadine – lovely white fizzy wine – at a lira per litro – quite a lot for fivepence, 3 or 4 tumblerfuls.

If we are here, could you come for the Easter vacation? Fancy, I might be alone. You could come 3rd quite cheaply, I should think. You would adore this country. How goes work? Have you seen Harold lately? I must write him. But I expected to hear again from him.

How's your heart? Still fluttering round a microscope?

Send me a book to read, will you? - a 4½d. that doesn't matter.

It is Easter in a month - good Lord! and so from hour to hour we ripe and ripe. Write and say something nice to us. 'What rhubarb, senna, or what purgative drug - etc.'

The theatre has gone, much to my sorrow. But good-bye - *viele herzliche Grüsse*.

D. H. LAWRENCE

14   TO EDWARD GARNETT

Villa Jaffé,
Irschenhausen,
(Post) Ebenhausen, bei München.
Friday, 17.4.13

DEAR GARNETT, -
I am sorry the poems only sold 100. - Frieda is very cross. Don't you think Duckworth's printers or somebody are very slow? If one wants things to go like hot cakes, the cakes should be hot, surely. But the poems hung fire for months - *Sons and Lovers* does likewise. The interest - what of it there may be - goes lukewarm. It's no good - if *Hamlet* and *Oedipus* were published now, they wouldn't sell more than 100 copies, unless they were pushed: I know that Duckworth will have to wait until my name is made, for his money. I can understand he is a bit diffident about putting me forward. But he needn't be afraid. I *know* I can write bigger stuff than any man in England. And I have to write what I can write. And I write for men like David and Harold - they will read me, soon. My stuff

is what they want: when they know what they want. You wait.

Bliss Carmen was very nice. I have half a mind to write to him. Shall I?

We – or rather Frieda – had a letter from Harold this morning.

I am only doing *reviews* for the *Blue Monthly*, or whatever it is.

Shall I send some poems, and a story, for the *Forum*?

I have written 180 pages of my newest novel, *The Sisters*. It is a queer novel, which seems to have come by itself. I will send it you. You may dislike it – it hasn't got hard outlines – and of course it's only first draft – but it is pretty neat, for me, in composition. Then I've got 200 pages of a novel which I'm saving – which is very lumbering – which I'll call, provisionally, *The Insurrection of Miss Houghton*. That I shan't send you yet, but it is, to me, fearfully exciting. It lies next my heart, for the present. But I am finishing *The Sisters*. It will only have 300 pages. It was meant to be for the *jeunes filles*, but already it has fallen from grace. I can only write what I feel pretty strongly about: and that, at present, is the relation between men and women. After all, it is *the* problem of today, the establishment of a new relation, or the readjustment of the old one, between men and women. In a month *The Sisters* will be finished (D.V.).

It is queer, but nobody seems to want, or to love, *two* people together. Heaps of folk love me alone – if I were alone – and of course all the world adores Frieda – when I'm not there. But together we seem to be a pest. I suppose married (*sic*) people ought to be sufficient to themselves. It's poverty which is so out of place.

I want to go back to Italy. I *have* suffered from the tightness, the *domesticity* of Germany. It is our domesticity which leads to our conformity, which chokes us. The very agricultural landscape here, and the distinct paths, stifles me. The very oxen are dull and featureless, and the folk seem like tables of figures. I have longed for Italy again, I can tell you.

I think these letters of ours are typical. Frieda sprawls so large I must squeeze myself small. I am very contractible. But aren't you writing a book about Dostoievsky? Those things crack my brains. How does it go? You *are* a pessimist really. We have *not* mentioned Mrs G. to anybody, I believe. Tell David to write to me here.

D. H. LAWRENCE

15   TO A. W. MCLEOD

Irschenhausen,
(Post) Ebenhausen, Oberbayern.
Wednesday

DEAR MAC, –

Thanks for the books. What a measly thing Shaw's *New Statesman* was. God help him! And it is amazing how narrowly Phillpotts shaves it, and *just* misses, always.

I sent you a rather miserable card of Wolfratshausen – thought it might interest you geographically. It looked rather nice on a white mount. *Sons and Lovers* comes out on the 29th. I've had just one copy – it looks nice. If they don't fall on me for morals, it should go. It is my best work, by far.

I have nearly done another remarkable work, called *The Sisters*. Oh, it is a wonder – but it wants dressing down a bit.

I am still sighing for Italy. Bavaria is too humid, too green and lush, and mountains *never* move – they are *always* there. They go all different tones and colours – but still, they are always there.

We are perhaps coming to England end of June – but not to stop. I hope to go back to Italy. Of course a lot depends on *Sons and Lovers* selling. You talk about the lines falling to me in pleasant places – I reckon a good many of 'em fall in stripes on my back. 'Resigned, I kissed the rod?' Never.

What did you do at Whitsuntide? I live in a green meadow by the budding pines, and look at these damned mountains, and write bloody rot. Oh, Gawd! Oh, Gawd!

There's a grand procession today – the folk in Bavaria are

the most fervent Roman Catholics on God's earth – and now it's come on in sheets of thunder-rain. It always does. Damned climate, this. I shall send you some of Arthur Ransome's *Essays*: ought to be entitled '*Je sais tout*'. Aren't you well? For the Lord's sake don't get ill, or I shall feel as if I heard the props of the earth cracking. I'll have a copy of *Sons and Lovers* sent you. Remember me to A. Where is he going for his summer holiday? And you? But I hope to see you before then.

Auf wiedersehen,

D. H. LAWRENCE

16   TO LADY CYNTHIA ASQUITH

Irschenhausen,
(Post) Ebenhausen,
Oberbayern.
Wed., Aug. 17, 1913, or thereabouts

DEAR MRS ASQUITH, –

Suddenly we've got a fit of talking about you and your skirt with holes in and your opal brooch. And again we are in the little cove by the sea – and it's absolutely heart-breaking to hear us singing the duet, *What are the wild waves saying?* I think I'm the living spit and image of Paul Dombey grown up, and Frieda – well, the less said about her the better.

You were awfully nice to us at Kingsgate. But that your Marylands was such a joy, I might have found myself hurrying over the edge of the cliff in my haste to get away from that half-crystallized nowhere of a place, Kingsgate. Kingsgate – oh, God! The last was a pathetic little bill for one and four-pence, the dregs and lees of our housekeeping down there. I believe it was the Baker. But it dogged our footsteps, and ran us down here. So I made a little boat of it and set it afloat. 'Cast thy bread upon the waters,' I cried to the Baker, 'and send thy bills out after it.' Far down the dancing Danube, and over Hungaria's restless plains, my Baker's bill on its bobbling course goes seeking the golden grains. Ask . . . if that isn't perfect Flecker-rhythm. *The Golden Journey to Samarcand.* You knew it climbed Parnassus *en route*? I shall write a book called *The Poet's Geographer* one day. By the way — will hold it as a personal favour if I will take more care of my rhythms. Poor things, they go cackling round like a poultry farm – but he told it me – in a letter. He thinks I'm too Rag-time! – not that he says so. But if you'll believe me, that *Golden Journey to Samarcand* only took place on paper – no matter who went to Asia Minor.

I hope you don't mind if my letter is rather incoherent. We live in a little wooden house (but genuine Dürer engravings and Persian rugs) in a corner of a pine forest. But it rains – oh Lord! – the rain positively stands up on end. Sometimes one sees the deer jumping up and down to get the wet out of their jackets, and the squirrels simply hang on by their tails, like washing. I take one morning run round the house in my bathing suit in lieu of a shower-bath.

It's Frieda's brother-in-law's house. He's staying here now and then. He's a professor of Political Economy, among other things. Outside the rain continues. We sit by lamplight and drink beer, and hear Edgar on Modern Capitalism. *Why* was I born? It was Markt in Wolfratshausen on Sunday. But there was nothing to buy but *Regenschirme* and *Hosentragen* and *debkuchen*. I wanted to buy a Herzkuchen with 'Frieda' on, but there was such a mob of young gents eagerly sorting them out – one wanted *Tauben* with Emilie and another *Vergissmichnicht* und *Creszenz*, so that I never got a look in. I am born to be elbowed out.

We are going to Italy in a month or so. Then we think of Lerici, somewhere near Leghorn – Shelley and Byron tradition. It might be good for my rhythms.

We had an awfully jolly lunch at Marsh's. I liked it ever so much.

How are you and where are you? Would you like any German books? – you can have some from here if you would – that was simply the best melon I ever tasted, the one you gave us. German books remind me of it.

How's the fat and smiling John? May I be remembered to Mr Asquith. My respects to the gallant Sir Walter and his Lady, if ever you see them.

Viele Grüsse,
D. H. Lawrence

Are you Honourable or aren't you? How does one address your letters?

17   To Edward Garnett

Albergo delle Palme,
Lerici, Golfo della Spezia,
Italy.
Tuesday, 30 Sept., 1913

Dear Garnett, –

I am so happy with the place we have at last discovered, I must write smack off to tell you. It is perfect. There is a little tiny bay half shut in by rocks, and smothered by olive woods that slope down swiftly. Then there is one pink, flat, fisherman's house. Then there is the villino of Ettore Gambrosier, a four-roomed pink cottage among vine gardens, just over the water and under the olive woods. There, D.V., is my next home. It is exquisite. One gets by rail from Genoa or from Parma to Spezia, by steamer across the gulf to Lerici, and by rowing boat round the headlands to Fiascherino, where is the villino which is to be mine. It is L60 a month – 60 lire, that is – furnished – and 25 lire for the woman who does all the work and washing and sleeps in Tellaro, the fishing village twenty minutes off; in all, 85 francs a month. You run out of the gate into the sea, which washes among the rocks at the mouth of the bay. The garden is all vines and fig trees, and great woods on the hills all round. Now you will come and see us – and so will Constanza Davidovna – she promised – she would be so happy. Yellow crocuses are out, wild. The Mediterranean

washes softly and nicely, with just a bit of white against the
rocks. Figs and grapes are ripe. You will come and see us –
and David too – it is a perfect place for him. Think, we can sit
round the open chimney in the kitchen at night, and burn olive
wood, and hear the sea washing. I want to go tomorrow. But
the proprietor remains in possession still another eight days,
for the crops. I feel I can't wait: Though this is a delicious
hotel – 6 francs a day pension, jolly good food, wine and all
included – a big bedroom with a balcony just over the sea,
very beautiful. But I want to go to my villino.

I haven't got much money left. The cheque from the *New
Statesman* hasn't come yet – but it will eventually wander here,
I suppose. Perhaps you could send me £10 from what I have
left. Send it me in notes here, to this Albergo.

I walked all the way from Schaffhausen to Zürich, Lucerne,
over the Gotthard to Airolo, Bellinzona, Lugano, Como. It
was beautiful – Switzerland too touristy, however – spoilt.

Don't ask me anything about literature this time.

Frieda's mother gave her a lot of this paper – please excuse it.

Love from both,
D. H. LAWRENCE

*Lerici, per Fiascherino,
Golfo della Spezia, Italy.*
23rd October, 1913

DEAR MRS ASQUITH, –

I have been wanting to write to you for such a long time.
But we have been 'on the way' here. It is ages since we left
Bavaria. Frieda went to her people in Baden Baden, which I
didn't want to do. So I walked across Switzerland – and am
cured of that little country for ever. The only excitement in it
is that you can throw a stone a frightfully long way down –

that is forbidden by law. As for mountains – if I stick my little finger over my head, I can see it shining against the sky and call it Monte Rosa. No, I can't do with mountains at close quarters – they are always in the way, and they are so stupid, never moving and never doing anything but obtrude themselves.

Then I got to beastly Milano, with its imitation hedgehog of a cathedral, and its hateful town Italians, all socks and purple cravats and hats over the ear, did for me.

But we've got an adorable place here, a beautiful palazzino in large grounds, that descend in terraces to the sea – that's the Italian for it. I call it a little pink four-roomed cottage in a big vine garden, on the edge of a rocky bay. Frieda calls it a pink-washed sepulchre, because it is – or was – so dirty inside. Lord, what a time we've had, scrubbing it. It was no use calling on Elide, the girl. She had never seen a scrubbing brush used. So I tied my braces round my waist and went for it. Lord, to see the dark floor flushing crimson, the dawn of deep red bricks rise from out this night of filth, was enough to make one burst forth into hymns and psalms. 'Ah,' cries Elide, 'l'aria e la pulizia – air and cleanliness are the two most important things in this life.' She might as well have said nectar and ambrosia, for all she knew of 'em.

But the Italians don't consider their houses, like we do, as being their extended persons. In England my house is my outer cuticle, as a snail has a shell. Here it is a hole into which I creep out of the rain and the dark. When they eat, the Capitano and his wife – the place belongs to them, she inherited it, but they let it and live in town – they fling all their scraps and 'bouts de vin' on the floor unceremoniously, and the cats and the flies do the war dance about them.

It's a lovely position – among the vines, a little pink house just above a rocky bay of the Mediterranean. One goes down in a towel to bathe. And the water is warm and buoyant – it *is* jolly. I wish you could try it too.

We live awfully cheaply – I know these things interest you more than eternal truths – house, 60 francs a month, maid 25, and vegetables in abundance, cheap as dirt. And in the morning one wakes and sees the pines all dark and mixed up with perfect rose of dawn, and all day long the olives shimmer in the sun, and fishing boats and strange sails like Corsican ships come out of nowhere on a pale blue sea, and then at evening all the sea is milky gold and scarlet with sundown. It is very pretty.

Did you make your dash to Venice – and did it stink? Lord, but how Italy can stink. We have to fetch letters from Tellaro – twenty-five minutes upstairs and downstairs on the sea-edge, an inaccessible little sea-robbers' place – and my dear heart, but it *is* dirty.

I hope you are pretty well – are you? But isn't it a bit much, to go dashing to Venice and back in a week? Why don't you go to Margate again? I think it makes an awful difference, when one is happy in a place. How is the Jonquil with the golden smile. Is Mr Asquith making heaps of money at the bar? I believe I'm going to get about £150 this winter, which will be rolling wealth for us here.

We heard from Eddie Marsh yesterday – such a heavy acorn fell on my head at this moment – now that is an omen. Are you any good at soothsaying? He is fearfully warm and generous, I think. I think I was wrong to feel injured because my verse wasn't well enough dished-up to please him.

The Mediterranean can get *very* cross. Today the wind is the Maelstrale – and the sea is showing its teeth in an unbecoming fashion.

I'm going to have a play published. The black hen has just come home. She went lost. Elide is waving her hands with joy. A very decent play. They won't give me any copies or I'd send you one. But you must read it.

My regards to Mr Asquith and to the Jonquil and to you.
Yours sincerely,
D. H. LAWRENCE

Lerici, per Fiascherino,
Golfo della Spezia, Italy.
Tuesday, Nov. — , 1913

DEAR MRS ASQUITH, –

Because I feel frightfully disagreeable, and not fit to con-
secrate myself to novels or to short stories, I'll write a letter. I
like to write when I feel spiteful; it's like having a good sneeze.
Don't mind, will you?

You say we're happy – per Bacchino! If you but knew the
thunderstorms of tragedy that have played over my wretched
head, as if I was set up on God's earth for a lightning conduc-
tor, you'd say, 'Thank God I'm not as that poor man'. If you
knew the slough of misery we've struggled and suffocated
through, you'd stroke your counterpane with a purring
motion, like an old maid having muffins for tea in the lamplight and reading *Stanley in Africa*. If ever you hear of me in a
mad-house, and Frieda buried under a nameless sod, you'll
say, 'Poor things, no wonder, with all they've gone through'.
You talk about tears drowning the wind – my God. We are
the most unfortunate, agonized, fate-harassed mortals since
Orestes and that gang. Don't you forget it. Put away all
illusions concerning us, and see the truth.

When I had an English feel come over me, I took it frightfully badly, that we had appeared before you as if we were a
perfectly respectable couple. I thought of the contamination –
etc., etc. – and I really was upset. I'm glad you didn't mind;
you might with justice have taken it amiss – and then, Lord,
what a state I should have been in when the English feel came
over me again. Heaven be blessed, England is only a spot of
grease on the soup just now.

I'm sorry you've got a cold. But what do you expect, after
purpling in Venice – Frieda's been in bed for four days also –
like Robinson Crusoe: 'First day, I vomited – .' I wandered
under the falling vines muttering: 'What rhubarb, senna and

what purgative drug – .' It was sheer misery. We *have* had a time, between us: oh dear o' me! She is a bit better today.

I've been to Spezia. Frieda *will* hire a piano, not a hurdy-gurdy. Well, it has to come first on the workmen's steamer to Lerici, then be got down into a rowing boat, and rowed along the coast, past jutting rocks where the sea goes up and down to bring your heart in your mouth, finally landed into the shingle of this little bay, and somehow got up the steps to the house. Well, the man found out what a journey it was, and he clings to his piano as if it were his only child, nor could I snatch it from him today. So we fell out – and in the midst of it a man in sailor's uniform with 'White Star' on his breast came and said he was English and did we want to buy contraband English cloth. And he wasn't English – nor French, nor German, nor Italian – but spoke twenty words of each. Now I might have wrested this pianoforte out of the fervent arms of Rugi Gulielmo, but for the interruption of the sailor with a sack. As it was, I returned, boat and all, empty save of curses.

'Ecco – un pianoforte – it's not like a piece of furniture – if it was a piece of furniture – he! va bene – but – a pianoforte – he! – '

I loathe and detest the Italians. They never argue, they just get hold of a parrot phrase, shove up their shoulders and put their heads on one side, and flap their hands. And what is an honest man to do with 'em? (Forget my past when I say 'Honest man'.) Now I shall have to go tomorrow, and pay a regiment of facchini to transport that cursed pianoforte.

> 'Take it up tenderly,
> Lift it with care,
> Fashioned so slenderly,
> Young and so fair.'

And it's a tin-pot thing not fit for a cat to walk up and down. And if it *does* go to the bottom of the sea – well, God bless it and peace be with it, a gay blonde head.

> 'Il pleut doucement sur la ville
> Comme il pleut dans mon cœur.'

As a matter of fact, it's a perfectly glittery and starry night, with a glow-worm outside the door, and on the sea a light-house beating time to the stars.

Well, adieu, fair lady, don't be cross and sad. Think that we have simply worn holes in our hankeys, with weeping.

Why should the cat sleep all night on my knee, and give me fleas to bear? Why?

There's a peasant wedding down below, next Saturday. The bride in white silk and orange blossom must clamber fearful roads, three hours there and back, to go to the Syndaco of l'Ameglia, to be married. Mass at 7.30 at Tellaro – *piccola colazione* at the bride's house at 8.30 – *un boccone* – marriage at 10.0 at l'Ameglia – *pranzo* down here at midday. We are invited. But it's rather sad, he doesn't want her very badly. One gets married – *si – come si fa!* They say it so often – *ma – come si fa!*

> Il pleut doucement dans la ville,
> I think I am missing a meal.

A rivederla, signoria,   D. H. LAWRENCE

They call us 'Signoria'. How's that for grandeur! Shades of my poor father!

20   TO W. E. HOPKIN

Lerici, per Fiascherino,
Golfo della Spezia, Italia.

18 *Dec.*, 1913

DEAR WILL, –

I *was* glad to get that letter from you, full of good old crusty Eastwood gossip. Always write to me like that.

And don't wonder at what I write now, for Felice is rattling away like a hail-storm in Italian, just near my left ear, and Frieda, with her usual softness of heart (and head now and then), is letting herself in for things that will need the courage of St George to extricate her from.

We *have* got a beautiful place here (and don't lose the address). It is a little pink cottage of four rooms, under great hills of olive woods, just over the sea. We have a great vine garden, all shut in, and lemons on the wall, and today, with a wind from the Apennines, the big, heavy oranges swing gold in their dark green leaves. We've only one orange tree, but it is a beauty.

There is no road here, that carts may pass – not even a mule road. Everything must go by rowing boat on the sea, that is not carried on the heads of the peasants. They carry, women and all, masses of stuff on their heads. It is supposed to give them a beautiful carriage, but that is a lie. It presses in the loins in a most curious fashion.

At this time of the year all the women are out in the olive woods – you have no idea how beautiful olives are, so grey, so delicately sad, reminding one constantly of the New Testament. I am always expecting when I go to Tellaro for the letters, to meet Jesus gossiping with his disciples as he goes along above the sea, under the grey, light trees. Now the hills are full of voices, the peasant women and children all day long and day after day, in the faint shadow of olives, picking the fallen fruit off the ground, pannier after pannier full. Our village is Tellaro. It grows sheer out of the rocks of the sea, a sea-robber's nest of 200 souls. The church is over the water. There is a tale that once in the night the church bell rang, and rang again. The people got up in terror – the bell rang mysteriously. Then it was found that the bell rope had fallen over the edge of the cliff in among the rocks, and an octopus had got hold of the end, and was drawing it. It is quite possible. The men go fishing for the octopus with a white bait and a long spear. They get quite big ones, six or seven pounds in weight sometimes – and you never saw anything so fiendishly ugly. But they are good to eat. We were at a peasant wedding the other day, and a great feast – octopus was one of the dishes: but I could not fancy it: I can eat snails all right, but octopus – no. We can have the boat belonging to the peasants on the bay when we like, and row out on the sea. The Mediterranean is quite wonderful – and when the sun sets beyond the islands of Porto Venere, and all the sea is like heaving white milk with a street of fire across it, and amethyst islands away back, it is too beautiful.

I am very fond of the Italians. We have a little oddity of a maid called Elide – 25 years old. Her old mother Felice is quite a figure. They are very funny and ceremonious. When Elide has put the soup on the table, she says '*a rivederci*, eh?' before she can leave us. There is only one other house on this bay – only one other house within nearly a mile – and that is the peasants' down on the beach. They are cousins of Elide. Sometimes they come and play and sing with us at evening – bringing the guitar. It is jolly. Luigi is very beautiful – and Gentile is a wild joy. How happy you would be with these people – and Mrs Hopkin with the country. The wind is now cold – there is snow on the mountains over Carrara – but still at night a glow-worm shines near the door, and sometimes a butterfly, a big black and red one, wanders to the remaining flowers – wild pinks and campanulas. I love living by the sea – one gets so used to its noise, one hears it no more. And the ships that pass, with many sails, to Sardinia and Sicily, and through the gates of Porto Venere to Genova, are very beautiful. Spezia is Italy's great naval arsenal. Right in the harbour lie her warships: and she wastes such a lot of powder with their rattling cannon. The men of the villages go into Spezia to work. The workmen run the only steamers across the bay. They are interesting.

And now, after all this, you must come – you and Mrs Hopkin at least – and Enid if she can. You can get here cheap, some way or other – perhaps by sea to Genoa or to Leghorn – or by trips. We shall be here, I think, till June. So make up your minds, and scrape together. I want you. We both *want* you to come – and it is the most beautiful place I know.

I am laughing at your swatting with Willie Dunn. We send heaps of good wishes for Christmas. Write to me oftener. And make up your minds to come. Mrs Hopkin promised us last spring.

Love from Frieda and me to you three.

Yrs,
D. H. LAWRENCE

Lerici, per Fiascherino,
Golfo della Spezia, Italy.
24 *Gennaio,* 1914

Dear Eddie,—

That *Georgian Poetry* book is a veritable Aladdin's lamp. I little thought my *Snapdragon* would go on blooming and seeding in this prolific fashion. So many thanks for the cheque for four pounds, and long life to *G. P.*

We are still trying to get over the excitement of your rush through Fiascherino. I still think with anguish of your carrying your bag up that salita from Lerici – don't remember it against me. I have received one or two more apologies from Severino, for his having taken us for the three *saltimbanchi:* the latter, by the way, gave a great performance in Tellaro, at the bottom there by the sea, on Sunday. They performed in the open air. Elide assisted at the spectacle, but confessed to disappearing into the church when the hat came round: along with three parts of the crowd. The poor *saltimbanchi* were reduced to begging for a little bread, so stingy was Tellaro.

The night you went, was a great fall of snow. We woke in the morning wondering what the queer pallor was. And the snow lay nearly six inches deep, and was still drifting finely, shadowily, out to the sombre-looking sea.

Of course, no Elide appeared. I got up and made a roaring fire and proceeded to wash the pots, in a queer, silent, muffled Fiascherino; even the sea was dead and still.

It looked very queer. The olives on the hills bowed low, low under the snow, so the whole slopes seemed peopled with despairing shades descending to the Styx. I never saw anything so like a host of bowed, pathetic despairers, all down the hillside. And every moment came the long creak – cre-eak of a tree giving way, and the crash as it fell.

The pines on the little peninsula were very dark and snowy, above a lead-grey sea. It was queer and Japanesy: no distance, no perspective, everything near and sharp on a dull grey ground. The water cut out a very perfect, sweeping curve from the snow on the beach.

The Mino – the cat – had been out at night as usual. He appeared shoulder-deep in snow, mewing, terrified – and he wouldn't come near me. He knows me perfectly. But that sudden fall of deep snow had frightened him out of his wits, and it was a long time before we could get him to come into the house.

At midday appeared Elide with her elder brother, Alessandro. *And* there was an outcry. Alessandro stood in the doorway, listening to the trees cracking, and crying, *'Ma dio, dio – senti signore, senti – Christo del mondo – è una rovina.'* All Tellaro was praying to the Vergine in the church: they had rung a special appeal at 9.30, and the old women had flocked in. Elide looked once more at the driving snow-flakes, stamped her foot like a little horse, and cried defiantly, *'Ma se il Dio vuol' mandare il fine del mondo – che lo manda.'* She was ready. Meanwhile Alessandro moaned, *'Una rovina, un danno!'*

It really was a ruin. Quite half the trees were smashed. One could not get out of our garden gate, for great trees fallen there. No post came to Tellaro – nothing happened but moaning. And the third day, in lamentation, they brought a commission to see the damage and to ask to have the taxes remitted. Now they are quite happily chopping up the ruin, crying, *'Ora si puo scaldarsi.'*

Another excitement! Luigi, down at the house on the bay here, the evening of your departure came home pale with excitement, found our Felice, and said hoarsely, *'Ma zia, io ho una brutta notizia da portare. Quelli due Inglesi del signore erano arrestati stasera, al pontino di Lerici.'* Loud, loud lamentations from Felice, Elide maintaining stoutly, *'Forse mancava qualche carta – di certo è una cosa di niente.'* Think how you let us in for it – between strolling players and arrests.

There was also a great argument between Felice and Elide, as to which of you was the more beautiful. Elide said Jim Barnes, Felice said you – and they got quite cross.

Addio,

D. H. LAWRENCE

Lerici, per Fiascherino,
Golfo della Spezia, Italy.
9th February, 1914

DEAR MAC,-

I must thank you first for the books. I think Crosland's
Sonnets are objectionable – he is a nasty person. I think Hilaire
Belloc is conceited. Full of that French showing-off which
goes down so well in England, and is so smartly shallow.
And I have always a greater respect for Mark Rutherford:
I *do* think he is jolly good – so thorough, so sound, and so
beautiful,

Tell me, when you write, what you thought of the poems
in *Poetry* and in the *English.* I am glad you sent me the former.
In England people have got that loathsome superior knack of
refusing to consider me a poet at all: 'Your prose is so good,'
say the kind fools, 'that we are obliged to forgive you your
poetry.' How I hate them. I believe they are still saying that
of Meredith. – In America they are not so priggish conceited.

I have begun my novel again – for about the seventh time.
I hope you are sympathizing with me. I had nearly finished it.
It was full of beautiful things, but it missed – I knew that it
just missed being itself. So here I am, must sit down and write
it out again. I know it is quite a lovely novel really – you know
that the perfect statue is in the marble, the kernel of it. But the
thing is the getting it out clean. I think I shall manage it pretty
well. You must say a prayer for me sometimes.

Mrs Garnett is staying at the hotel in Lerici, with a Russian
girl. She was speaking of you the other day, how sorry she
was she did not see anything of you. Why don't you go and
see them sometimes?

Kennerley says they have sent me my plays from New York,
but they haven't come yet. I look forward to having them.
You must have patience with my promise of one. – By the

way, what a frightfully *decent* paper the *Morning Post* is. The more I read it, the more I think it is worth while to be a gentleman and to have to do with gentlemen. Their reviews of books, their leaders, and all, have such a decent, honourable tone, such a relief after the majority of newspaper filth.

We have got spring coming in already. I have found a handful of the little wild narcissus, with the yellow centres, and a few sweet violets, and a few purplish crimson anemones with dark centres. And one can drift about all afternoon in the boat, getting shell-fish from off the rocks under water, with a long split cane. You know that warm, drowsy, uneasy feel of spring, when scents rouse up. It is already here. And the lizards are whipping about on the rocks, like a sudden flicking of a dried grass blade. And one is wakened in the morning by the birds singing. They are almost brave – they sing aloud as the sun comes up, in spite of the bold Italian *cacciatore*, who, in full costume and a long slim gun, stalks shadowily through the olive trees in quest of wrens and robins. When I walked in Switzerland, and came across a colony of Italians in a public-house –

'*L'Italia – ah che bel sole! – e gli uccellini – ! !*' 'Oh, Italy – such a beautiful sun – and the little birds – aren't they *good!*' – the cry of the exile.

Frieda sends warmest regards – *une bonne poignée.*

D. H. LAWRENCE

23   TO A. W. MCLEOD

Lerici, per Fiascherino,
Golfo della Spezia, Italia.
14 *Marzo,* 1914

DEAR MAC, –

Thanks for the *House of the Dead*. We have begun reading it, but I don't like it *very* much. It seems a bit dull: so much *statement*.

It reminds me that the other Sunday we went to the house of a very popular modern Russian novelist, Amphiteatroff, at Levanto. It *was* a rum show: twenty-six people at lunch, a babble of German, English, Russian, French, Italian – a great fat laughing man, the host, carefully judging the Cinque Terre wine: a drawing-room, clever, highly educated wife at the head of the table, a peasant sculptor in a peasant's smock at the foot, and in between a motley of tutors and music teachers for the children – an adopted son of Maxim Gorky, little, dark, agile, full of life, and a great wild Cossack wife whom he had married for passion and had come to hate – then a house full of scuffling servants and cultured children – no, it was too much. You have no idea how one feels English and stable and solid in comparison. I felt as if my head were screwed on tighter than the foundations of the world, in comparison. I must say, in one way, I loved them – for their absolute carelessness about everything but just what interested them. They are fine where we have become stupid.

Oh, it is so beautiful here, I feel as if my heart would jump out of my chest like a hare at night – it is such lovely spring. The sea is blue all day, and primrose dusking to apricot at evening. There are flowers, and peach trees in bloom, and pink almond trees among the vapour grey of the olives.

Today we have been a great picnic high up, looking at the Carrara mountains, and the flat valley of the Magra, and the sea coast sweeping round in a curve that makes my blood run with delight, sweeping round, and it seems up into the vaporous heaven with tiny scattering of villages, like handfuls of shells thrown on the beach, right beyond Viareggio. – I could not tell you how I could jump up into the air, it is so lovely. I want at this time to walk away, to walk south, into the Apennines, through the villages one sees perched high up across the valley.

My novel goes on slowly. It ought to be something when it is done, the amount of me I have given it.

I think there will be some of my poems in a paper called *The Egoist*. I don't know anything about it. Ezra Pound took some verses, and sent me £3 3s. Try to get a copy, will you? – I believe it will be next month – it might be this, but I think not. But unless I can get hold of a copy I absolutely don't know what they have published.

I wish you could come here – why don't you try?

Many regards from us both. Don't you keep on sending us things, it seems such an imposition. Did you get the copy of the play I sent you? Tell me what you think of it – I wait to hear – *tanti saluti*.

D. H. LAWRENCE

24   TO J. M. MURRY

Lerici, per Fiascherino,
Golfo della Spezia,
Italy.

8 Maggio, 1914

DEAR MURRY, –

I wrote to Katherine yesterday, but don't know if she'll get the letter, as the address is different.

As a matter of fact, all you ought to do is to get well physically and let everything else go. You say you are patient – now use your patience for letting your soul alone and making your body well. You make one as miserable as miserable. Do for God's sake lie down and leave everything to other people just now. Don't bother – things are all right, really. Let them work out themselves. Don't give up feeling that people *do* want to hear what you say; or rather, they don't *want* to hear, but they need to, poor things. Don't be so miserable. Have patience with yourself most of all. Don't be miserable. You've used too much of your strength, and now you're weak, and will have to depend on other people for a bit. But I am *sure* you are the best critic in England; I'm *sure* you can help terrifically to a new, cleaner outlook. But you can't do anything if you squander yourself in these miseries. Do consent to be poor and dependent – what does it matter?

The play (*Mrs Holroyd*) – well, it's not bad. I don't set great store by it. I will send you a copy when Duckworth will give me some. I will write and ask him to send you a copy. It isn't worth 3/6 of your money, at any rate.

Four days, and I shall have finished my novel, pray God. Don't get sick and leave me in the lurch over it. Can you understand how cruelly I feel the want of friends who will believe in me a bit? People think I'm a sort of queer fish that can write; that is all, and how I loathe it. There isn't a soul cares a damn for me, except Frieda – and it's rough to have all the burden put on her.

We are coming to London in June. Till the divorce was pronounced, we only allowed a mere possibility of England this summer. We thought of going to Germany from here. But now Frieda is set on England in June – we shall come in about a month's time. For what will happen then, we must pray heaven. But I only decided to come two days ago.

I'm glad I shall see you again soon. We must try and be decent to each other all round. I wish you had come out here instead of going to Paris. Never mind. Do get better, and leave things.

Frieda sends many sympathies. We shall see you soon.

Yrs,

D. H. LAWRENCE

25   To T. D. D.

The Cearne,
Near Edenbridge,
Kent.

7 July, 1914

DEAR D., –

I was glad to get your still sad letter, and sorry you are so down yet. I can't help thinking that you wouldn't be quite so down if you and Mrs D. didn't let yourselves be separated rather by this trouble. Why do you do that? I think the trouble ought to draw you together, and you seem to let it put you apart. Of course I may be wrong. But it seems a shame that her one cry, when she is in distress, should be for her mother. You ought to be the mother and father to her. Perhaps if you go away to your unhealthy post, it may be good for you. But perhaps you may be separating your inner life from hers – I don't mean anything actual and external – but you may be taking yourself inwardly apart from her, and leaving her inwardly separate from you: which is no true marriage, and is a form of failure. I am awfully sorry; because I think that no amount of outward trouble and stress of circumstance could really touch you both, if you were together. But if you are not together, of course, the strain becomes too great, and you want to be alone, and she wants her mother. And it seems to me an awful pity if, after you have tried, you have to fail and go separate ways. I am not speaking of vulgar outward separation: I know you would always be a good reliable husband: but there is more than that: there is the real sharing of one life. I can't help thinking your love for Mrs D. hasn't quite been vital enough to give you yourself peace. One must learn to love, and go through a good deal of suffering to get to it, like any knight of the grail, and the journey is always *towards* the other soul, not away from it. Do you think love is an accomplished thing, the day it is recognized? It isn't. To love, you have to learn to understand the other, more than she understands herself, and to submit to her understanding of you. It is damnably difficult and painful, but it is the only thing which endures. You mustn't think that your desire or your fundamental need is to make a good career, or to fill your life with activity, or even to provide for your family materially. It isn't. Your most vital necessity in this life is that you shall love your wife completely and implicitly and in entire nakedness of body and spirit. Then you will have peace and inner security, no matter how many things go wrong. And this peace and security will leave you free to act and to produce your own work, a real independent workman.

You asked me once what my message was. I haven't got any

general message, because I believe a general message is a general means of side-tracking one's own personal difficulties: like Christ's – thou shalt love thy neighbour as thyself – has given room for all the modern filthy system of society. But this that I tell you is my message as far as I've got any.

Please don't mind what I say – you know I don't really want to be impertinent or interfering.

Mrs Huntingdon is coming over to England this month. Probably she would bring Mrs D. But perhaps Noémi would be better. I am sorry Paddy is still so seedy. He is a strange boy. I think he will need a lot of love. He has a curious heavy consciousness, a curious awareness of what people feel for him. I think he will need a lot of understanding and a lot of loving. He may, I think, have quite an unusual form of intelligence. When you said he might be a musician, it struck me. He has got that curious difference from other people, which may mean he is going to have a distinct creative personality. But he will suffer a great deal, and he will want a lot of love to make up for it.

I think our marriage comes off at the Kensington registrar's office on Saturday. I will try to remember to send you the *Times* you asked for. When I get paid for my novel, I want to send you a small cheque for doing the novel. You will not mind if it is not very much that I send you.

We are very tired of London already, and very glad to be down here in the country. Probably we are going to stay in Derbyshire – and then for August going to the west of Ireland. But I shall write and tell you. Don't be miserable – I have you and Mrs D. rather on my conscience just now – I feel as if you were taking things badly. But don't do that.

Auf wiedersehen,

D. H. LAWRENCE

Remember me to Mrs D.

The Triangle,
Bellingdon Lane,
Chesham,
Bucks.

1 Oct., 1914

DEAR HARRIET MONROE, –

I'm glad to hear my *Ophelia* shall go in whole – a great relief to me. I could not bear that she should be cut through the middle, and the top half given to me and the lower half given to the world. Am I not her mother, you Solomon with the sword?

Send me the draft here, to this God-forsaken little hole where I sit like a wise rabbit with my pen behind my ear, and listen to distant noises. I am not in the war zone. I think I am much too valuable a creature to offer myself to a German bullet gratis and for fun. Neither shall I go in for your war poem. The nearest I could get to it would be in the vein of

> The owl and the pussy cat went to sea
> In a beautiful peagreen boat

– and I know you wouldn't give me the hundred dollars.

I will let you know if I change my address.

Yours sincerely,
D. H. LAWRENCE

27   To EDWARD GARNETT

Bellingdon Lane,
Chesham, Bucks.

13 *Oct.,* 1914

DEAR GARNETT, –

It is a long time since I have written, but the war puts a damper on one's own personal movement. It makes me feel very abstract, as if I and what I am did not matter very much.

What are you doing? Do you still go as usual to Duckworth's? Or is there not so much work to do.

The proofs of the stories keep on coming. What *good* printers these Plymouth people are. They never make a mistake. And how good my stories are, after the first two. It really surprises me. Shall they be called *The Fighting Line*? After all, this is the real fighting line, not where soldiers pull triggers.

We hear now and then from Germany: every German heart full of the altar-fire of sacrifice to the war: two of the Richthofen intimate officer-friends killed, 'der gute Udo von Henning ist am 7. Sept. bei Charleroi gefallen' – that is the spirit. Frieda's father is very ill. She and I hardly quarrel any more.

We have a little money – not much – enough – Pinker sold *Honour and Arms* to America for £25, and I had a little from the *Manchester Guardian*. Here the autumn has been very beautiful. We are quite isolated, amid wide, grassy roads, with quantities of wild autumn fruit. This is curiously pale-tinted country, beautiful for the blueness and mists of autumn.

I have been writing my book more or less – very much less – about Thomas Hardy, I have done a third of it. When this much is typed I shall send it to Bertram Christian.

I wonder if you will come and see us. I should be very glad. It is not dear – there are cheap week-end tickets. And why doesn't David come?

Come for a week-end, will you? We have a bed. Any week-end after this next.

Our love to Mrs Garnett,

D. H. LAWRENCE

Greatham, Pulborough,
Sussex.
Sunday, 30th January, 1915

Dear Lady Cynthia, –

We were very glad to hear from you. I wanted to send you a copy of my stories at Christmas, then I didn't know how the war had affected you – I knew Herbert Asquith was joined and I thought you'd rather be left alone, perhaps.

We have no history, since we saw you last. I feel as if I had less than no history – as if I had spent those five months in the tomb. And now, I feel very sick and corpse-cold, too newly risen to share yet with anybody, having the smell of the grave in my nostrils, and a feel of grave clothes about me.

The War finished me: it was the spear through the side of all sorrows and hopes. I had been walking in Westmorland, rather happy, with water-lilies twisted round my hat – big, heavy, white and gold water-lilies that we found in a pool high up – and girls who had come out on a spree and who were having tea in the upper room of an inn, shrieked with laughter. And I remember also we crouched under the loose wall on the moors and the rain flew by in streams, and the wind came rushing through the chinks in the wall behind one's head, and we shouted songs, and I imitated music-hall turns, whilst the other men crouched under the wall and I pranked in the rain on the turf in the gorse, and Koteliansky groaned Hebrew music – Tiranenu Zadikim b'adonai.

It seems like another life – we *were* happy – four men. Then we came down to Barrow-in-Furness, and saw that war was declared. And we all went mad. I can remember soldiers kissing on Barrow station, and a woman shouting defiantly to her sweetheart – 'When you get at 'em, Clem, let 'em have it,' as the train drew off – and in all the tramcars, 'War'. Messrs Vickers-Maxim call in their workmen – and the great notices on Vickers' gateways – and the thousands of men streaming over the bridge. Then I went down the coast a few miles. And I think of the amazing sunsets over flat sands and the smoky sea – then of sailing in a fisherman's boat, running in the wind against a heavy sea – and a French onion boat coming in with her sails set splendidly, in the morning sunshine – and the electric suspense everywhere – and the amazing, vivid, visionary beauty of everything, heightened by the immense pain everywhere. And since then, since I came back, things have not existed for me. I have spoken to no one, I have touched no one, I have seen no one. All the while, I swear, my soul lay in the tomb – not dead, but with a flat stone over it, a corpse, become corpse-cold. And nobody existed, because I did not exist myself. Yet I was not dead – only passed over – trespassed – and all the time I knew I should have to rise again.

Now I am feeble and half alive. On the Downs on Friday I opened my eyes again, and saw it was daytime. And I saw the sea lifting up and shining like a blade with the sun on it. And high up, in the icy wind, an aeroplane flew towards us from the land – and the men ploughing and the boys in the fields on the table-lands, and the shepherds, stood back from their work and lifted their faces. And the aeroplane was small and high, in the thin, ice-cold wind. And the birds became silent and dashed to cover, afraid of the noise. And the aeroplane floated high out of sight. And below, on the level earth away down – were floods and stretches of snow, and I knew I was awake. But as yet my soul is cold and shaky and earthy.

I don't feel so hopeless now I am risen. My heart has been as cold as a lump of dead earth, all this time, because of the War. But now I don't feel so dead. I feel hopeful. I couldn't tell you how fragile and tender this hope is – the new shoot of life. But I feel hopeful now about the War. We should all rise again from this grave – though the killed soldiers will have to wait for the last trump.

There is my autobiography – written because you ask me, and because, being risen from the dead, I know we shall all come through, rise again and walk healed and whole and new in a big inheritance, here on earth.

It sounds preachy, but I don't quite know how to say it.

Viola Meynell has lent us this rather beautiful cottage. We are quite alone. It is at the foot of the Downs. I wish you would come and see us, and stay a day or two. It is quite comfortable – there is hot water and a bathroom, and two spare bedrooms. I don't know when we shall be able to come to London. We are too poor for excursions. But we *should* like to see you, and it *is* nice here.

D. H. LAWRENCE

Greatham, Pulborough, Sussex.
March, 1915

MY DEAR LADY OTTOLINE,–

I send you the next batch of the MS. There will only be one more lot. I hope you will like it.

Monica has a motor-car every day to drive her out, so we go too. Today we drove to Bognor. It was strange at Bognor – a white, vague, powerful sea, with long waves falling heavily, with a crash of frosty white out of the pearly whiteness of the day, of the wide sea. And the small boats that were out in the distance heaved, and seemed to glisten shadowily. Strange the sea was, so strong. I saw a soldier on the pier, with only one leg. He was young and handsome: and strangely self-conscious, and slightly ostentatious: but confused. As yet, he does not realize anything, he is still in the shock. And he is strangely roused by the women, who seem to have a craving for him. They look at him with eyes of longing, and they want to talk to him. So he is roused, like a roused male, yet there is more wistfulness and wonder than passion or desire. I could see him under chloroform having the leg amputated. It was still in his face. But he was brown and strong and handsome.

It seemed to me anything might come out of that white, silent, opalescent sea; and the great icy shocks of foam were strange. I felt as if legions were marching in the mist. I cannot tell you why, but I am afraid. I am afraid of the ghosts of the dead. They seem to come marching home in legions over the white, silent sea, breaking in on us with a roar and a white iciness. Perhaps this is why I feel so afraid. I don't know. But the land beyond looked warm, with a warm, blue sky, very homely: and over the sea legions of white ghosts tramping. I was on the pier.

So they are making a Coalition government. I cannot tell you how icy cold my heart is with fear. It is as if we were all going to die. Did I not tell you my revolution would come? It will come, God help us. The ghosts will bring it. Why does one feel so coldly afraid? Why does even the coalition of the Government fill me with terror? Some say it is for peace negotiations. It may be, because we are all afraid. But it is most probably for conscription. The touch of death is very cold and horrible on us all.

D. H. LAWRENCE

It is the whiteness of the ghost legions that is so awful.

30   TO LADY OTTOLINE MORRELL

Greatham, Pulborough, Sussex.
14 *May*, 1915

MY DEAR LADY OTTOLINE,—

I wonder if you are still in Buxton, and if you got the last batch of MS. which I sent you, enclosed with a copy of the *Imagist Anthology* which contains some of my verses. If you got them, tell me, will you?

We were in London for four days: beautiful weather, but I don't like London. My eyes can see nothing human that is good, nowadays: at any rate, nothing public. London seems to me like some hoary massive underworld, a hoary ponderous inferno. The traffic flows through the rigid grey streets like the rivers of hell through their banks of dry, rocky ash. The fashions and the women's clothes are very ugly.

Coming back here, I find the country very beautiful. The apple trees are leaning forwards, all white with blossom, towards the green grass. I watch, in the morning when I wake up, a thrush on the wall outside the window – not a thrush, a blackbird – and he sings, opening his beak. It is a strange thing to watch his singing, opening his beak and giving out his calls and warblings, then remaining silent. He looks so remote, so buried in primeval silence, standing there on the wall, and bethinking himself, then opening his beak to make the strange, strong sounds. He seems as if his singing were a sort of talking to himself, or of thinking aloud his strongest thoughts. I wish I was a blackbird, like him. I hate men.

> 'The ousel cock of sable hue
> And orange-yellow bill.'

The bluebells are all out in the wood, under the new vivid leaves. But they are rather dashed aside by yesterday's rain. It would be nice if the Lord sent another flood and drowned the world. Probably I should want to be Noah. I am not sure.

I've got again into one of those horrible sleeps from which I can't wake. I can't brush it aside to wake up. You know those horrible sleeps when one is struggling to wake up, and can't. I was like it all autumn – now I am again like it. Everything has a touch of delirium, the blackbird on the wall is a delirium, even the apple-blossom. And when I see a snake winding rapidly in the marshy places, I think I am mad.

It is not a question of me, it is the world of men. The world of men is dreaming, it has gone mad in its sleep, and a snake is strangling it, but it can't wake up.

When I read of the *Lusitania*, and of the riots in London, I know it is so. I think soon we must get up and try to stop it. Let us wait a little longer. Then when we cannot bear it any longer, we must try to wake up the world of men, which has gone mad in its sleep.

I cannot bear it much longer, to let the madness get stronger and stronger possession. Soon we in England shall go fully mad, with hate. I too hate the Germans so much, I could kill every one of them. Why should they goad us to this frenzy of hatred, why should we be tortured to – madness, when we are only grieved in our souls, and heavy? They will drive our heaviness and our grief away in a fury of rage. And we don't want to be worked up into this fury, this destructive madness of rage. Yet we must, we are goaded on and on. I am mad with rage myself. I would like to kill a million Germans – two millions.

I wonder when we shall see you again, and where you are. I have promised to stay here for another month at least, to teach Mary Saleeby. Her mother has a nervous breakdown, and they asked me to teach the child. I do it for the child's sake, for nothing else. So my mornings are taken up, for $3\frac{1}{2}$ hours each day.

Don't take any notice of my extravagant talk – one must say something. Write soon and tell us where you are, and how you are. I feel a little bit anxious about you, when you do not write.

Vale!

D. H. LAWRENCE

31   To LADY OTTOLINE MORRELL.

Greatham, Pulborough, Sussex.

Sunday

MY DEAR LADY OTTOLINE, –

I send you what is done of my philosophy. Tell me what you think, exactly.

Bertie Russell is here. I feel rather glad at the bottom, because we are rallying to a point. I do want him to work in the knowledge of the Absolute, in the knowledge of eternity. He *will* – apart from philosophical mathematics – be so temporal, so immediate. He won't let go, he won't act in the eternal things, when it comes to men and life. He is coming to have a real, actual, logical belief in Eternity, and upon this he can work: a belief in the absolute, an existence in the Infinite. It is very good and I am very glad.

We think to have a lecture hall in London in the autumn, and give lectures: he on Ethics, I on Immortality: also to have meetings, to establish a little society or body around a *religious belief, which leads to action*. We must centre in the knowledge of the Infinite, of God. Then from this centre each one of us must work to put the temporal things of our own natures and of our own circumstances in accord with the Eternal God we know. You must be president. You must preside over our meetings. You must be the centre-pin that holds us together, and the needle which keeps our direction constant, always towards the Eternal thing. We *mustn't* lapse into temporality.

Murry must come in, and Gilbert – and perhaps Campbell. We can all lecture, at odd times. Murry has a genuine side to his nature: so has Mrs Murry. Don't mistrust them. They are valuable, I know.

We must have some meetings at Garsington. Garsington must be the retreat where we come together and knit ourselves together. Garsington is wonderful for that. It is like the Boccaccio place where they told all the Decamerone. That wonderful lawn, under the ilex trees, with the old house and its exquisite old front – it is so remote, so perfectly a small world to itself, where one *can* get away from the temporal things to consider the big things. We must draw together. Russell and I have really got somewhere. We must bring the Murrys in. Don't be doubtful of them; and Frieda will come round soon. It is the same thing with her as with all the Germans – all the world – she hates the Infinite – my immortality. But she will come round.

I *know* what great work there is for us all to do in the autumn and onwards. Mind you keep your strength for it and we must really put aside the smaller personal things, and really live together in the big impersonal world as well: that must be our real place of assembly, the immortal world, the heaven of the great angels.

Send my philosophy on to Gilbert, will you? And tell me if you like it.

Don't be sad. We are only sad for a little while. At the bottom one *knows* the eternal things, and is glad.

My love to Julian and to you. My warm regards to Morrell – remember me to Maria, and to Miss Sands, and Miss Hudson. I trust in you entirely in this eternal belief.

D. H. LAWRENCE

32   TO LADY CYNTHIA ASQUITH

Littlehampton.

Tuesday

MY DEAR LADY CYNTHIA, –

We have lived a few days on the seashore, with the wave banging up at us. Also over the river, beyond the ferry, there is the flat silvery world, as in the beginning, untouched: with pale sand, and very much white foam, row after row, coming from under the sky, in the silver evening: and no people, no people at all, no houses, no buildings, only a haystack on the edge of the shingle, and an old black mill. For the rest, the flat unfinished world running with foam and noise and silvery light, and a few gulls swinging like a half-born thought. It is a great thing to realize that the original world is still there – perfectly clean and pure, many white advancing foams, and only the gulls swinging between the sky and the shore; and in the wind the yellow sea poppies fluttering very hard, like yellow gleams in the wind, and the windy flourish of the seed-horns.

It is this mass of unclean world that we have superimposed on the clean world that we cannot bear. When I looked back, out of the clearness of the open evening, at this Littlehampton dark and amorphous like a bad eruption on the edge of the land, I was so sick I felt I could not come back: all these little amorphous houses like an eruption, a disease on the clean earth; and all of them full of such a diseased spirit, every landlady harping on her money, her furniture, every visitor harping on his latitude of escape from money and furniture. The whole thing like an active disease, fighting out the health. One watches them on the sea-shore, all the people, and there is something pathetic, almost wistful in them, as if they wished that their lives did *not* add up to this scaly nullity of possession, but as if they could not escape. It is a dragon that has devoured us all: these obscene, scaly houses, this insatiable struggle and desire to possess, to possess always and in spite of everything, this need to be an owner, lest one be owned. It is too horrible. One can no longer live with people: it is too hideous and nauseating. Owners and owned, they are like the two sides of a ghastly disease. One feels a sort of madness come over one, as if the world had become hell. But it is only superimposed: it is only a temporary disease. It can be cleaned away . . .

One must destroy the spirit of money, the blind spirit of possession. It is the dragon for your St George: neither rewards on earth nor in heaven, of ownership: but always the give and take, the fight and the embrace, no more, no diseased stability of possessions, but the give and take of love and conflict, with the eternal consummation in each. The only permanent thing is *consummation* in love or hate.

D. H. LAWRENCE

33   To W. E. HOPKIN

1, Byron Villas,
Vale of Health,
Hampstead, London.
14 Sept., 1915

MY DEAR WILLIE, –

We have taken a little flat here, and are to spend the winter in town. If ever you can get up to London, you or Sallie, or Enid, we can rig you up a bed. We shall be very glad to see you.

I send you some leaflets about our paper. It is a rash venture. We are desperately poor, but we must do something, so we are taking the responsibility of this little journal on ourselves, Murry and I, and also we are going to have meetings in a room in town – 12, Fisher St – which we have taken. Heaven knows what will come of it: but this is my first try at direct approach to the public: art after all is indirect and ultimate. I want this to be more immediate.

Get me a few people in Sheffield, will you – people who care vitally about the freedom of the soul – a few people anywhere – but only those who really care. Ask Sallie to write to Mrs Dax – I would rather not open a correspondence with her again, after so long a silence; though I like her, and always shall feel her an integral part of my life; but that is in the past, and the future is separate. Yet I want her to have this paper, which will contain my essential beliefs, the ideas I struggle with. And perhaps she – Alice Dax – will ask one or two people in Liverpool, Blanche Jennings, for instance. You see I want to initiate, if possible, a new movement for real life and real freedom. One can but try.

I wish we could meet and talk. Soon I shall go to Ripley. Perhaps you will come to London. I send you the proofs of a story that is coming in next month's *English Review*.

Tell Sallie I feel she *must* come and see this *tiny* flat on Hampstead Heath.

Greetings from Frieda, and love from me.

D. H. LAWRENCE

34   To LADY CYNTHIA ASQUITH

1 Byron Villas,
Vale of Health,
Hampstead, London.
21st October, 1915

MY DEAR LADY CYNTHIA, –

What can one say about your brother's death except that it *should not be*. How long will the nations continue to empty the future – it is your own phrase – think what it means – I am sick in my soul, sick to death. But not angry any more, only unfathomably miserable about it all. I think I shall go away to

America if they will let me. In this war, in the whole spirit which we now maintain, I do *not* believe, I believe it is *wrong*, so awfully wrong, that it is like a great consuming fire that draws up all our souls in its draught. So if they will let me I shall go away soon, to America. Perhaps you will say it is cowardice: but how shall one submit to such ultimate wrong as this which we commit, now, England – and the other nations? If thine eye offend thee, pluck it out. And I am English, and my Englishness is my very vision. But now I must go away, if my soul is sightless for ever. Let it then be blind, rather than commit the vast wickedness of acquiescence.

Don't think I am not sorry about your brother – it makes me tremble. Don't think I want to hurt you – or anybody – I would do anything rather. But now I feel like a blind man who would put his eyes out rather than stand witness to a colossal and deliberate horror.

Yours,
D. H. LAWRENCE

I am so sorry for your mother. I can't bear it. If only the women would get up and speak with authority.

35   TO J. B. PINKER

1, Byron Villas,
Vale of Health,
Hampstead, London.
6 Nov., 1915

DEAR PINKER, –
I had heard yesterday about the magistrates and *The Rainbow*. I am not very much moved: am beyond that by now. I only curse them all, body and soul, root, branch and leaf, to eternal damnation.

As for Hübsch, if you think it is a good and wise proceeding for him to publish the book in America, then let him publish it. But please tell him all that has happened here.

I am away from Monday to Thursday of next week. If there is anything to write to me, address me at
Garsington Manor,
Near Oxford.
I will come and see you on Friday, if that suits you. Perhaps you will offer me that lunch then: otherwise one day early the next week.

I hope to be going away in about a fortnight's time: to America: there is a man who more or less offers us a cottage in Florida: but nothing is settled yet. We have got passports. It is the end of my writing for England. I will try to change my public.

Yours,
D. H. LAWRENCE

36   TO LADY CYNTHIA ASQUITH

1, *Byron Villas,*
Vale of Health
Hampstead, London.
28th November, 1915

MY DEAR LADY CYNTHIA, —
You ask me to send you our news: but as there isn't any there's no excuse for writing. People are desultorily working about the *Rainbow:* I am struggling like a fly on a treacle paper, to leave this country. I am hoping to be able to scrape together a little money, so that we can go to Florida straight, instead of going first to New York. I don't want to go to New York — not yet, not now. I would like to go to a land where there are only birds and beasts and no humanity, nor inhumanity-masks.

This is the plan and the prospect. A man will find out about a trading ship going to the Gulf of Mexico. We sail in this — soon. Then, if possible, we make for our destination in Florida — Fort Myers.

Fort Myers is a little town (5000) half negro – 9 miles from sea, on a wide river 1½ miles wide – backed by orange groves and pine forests. An American here will give us letters of introduction to friends there. That is the plan. I hope to find the ship and to sail before Christmas. There is the other point – whether the English Government will let me go – I have had far too much already.

For the rest of the news: tomorrow we are going to Garsington for a day or two. I've got a new suit and Frieda has got a new coat and skirt. I have made her a hat, a sort of Russian toque – out of bits of fur – so she looks very nice. She is also going to have a big warm coat, because it is so cold.

My heart is quartered into a thousand fragments, and I shall never have the energy to collect the bits – like Osiris – or Isis. In Florida I shall swallow a palm seed, and see if that'll grow a new heart for me.

I want to begin all over again. All these Gethsemane Calvary and Sepulchre stages must be over now: there must be a resurrection – resurrection: a resurrection with sound hands and feet and a whole body and a new soul: above all, a new soul: a resurrection. It is finished and ended, and put away, and forgotten, and translated to a new birth, this life, these thirty years. There must be a new heaven and a new earth, and a new heart and soul: all new: a pure resurrection.

> Now like a crocus in the autumn time,
> My soul comes naked from the falling night
> Of death, a Cyclamen, a Crocus flower
> Of windy autumn when the winds all sweep
> The hosts away to death, where heap on heap
> The leaves are smouldering in a funeral wind.

That is the first poem I have written for many a day – a bit of it – there's much more. They burn the leaves in heaps on the Heath – and the leaves blow in the wind, then the smoke: and the leaves are like soldiers.

I don't know why on earth I say these things to you: why you sort of ask me. But the conscious life – which you adhere to – is no more than a masquerade of death: there is a living unconscious life. If only we would shut our eyes; if only we were all struck blind, and things vanished from our sight, we should marvel that we had fought and lived for shallow, visionary, peripheral nothingnesses. We should find reality in the darkness.

Sometimes I am angry that I write these letters to you – but then I'm often angry. I suppose you *do* really care about the difference between life and death. *Vale!*

D. H. LAWRENCE

37   TO KATHERINE MANSFIELD

1, *Byron Villas,*
Vale of Health,
Hampstead.
Monday, 20 *Dec.,* 1915

MY DEAR KATHERINE, –

Your letter came this morning. I am so sorry you are so ill. Yesterday Murry was here when the letter came – Kot brought it – and he was much upset.

Do not be sad. It is one life which is passing away from us, one 'I' is dying; but there is another coming into being, which is the happy, creative you. I knew you would have to die with your brother; you also, go down into death and be extinguished. But for us there is a rising from the grave, there is a resurrection, and a clean life to begin from the start, new, and happy. Don't be afraid, don't doubt it, it is so.

You have gone further into your death than Murry has. He runs away. But one day he too will submit, he will dare to go down, and be killed, to die in this self which he is. Then he will become a man; not till. He is not a man yet.

When you get better, you must come back and we will begin afresh, it will be the first struggling days of spring, after winter. Our lives have been all autumnal and wintry. Now it is mid-winter. But we are strong enough to give way, to pass away, and to be born again.

I want so much that we should create a life in common, a new spirit, a spirit of unanimity between a few of us who are desirous in spirit, that we should add our lives together, to make one tree, each of us free and producing in his separate fashion, but all of us together forming one spring, a unanimous blossoming. It needs that we be one in spirit, that is all. What we are personally is of second importance.

And it is in its inception, this new life. From the old life, all is gone. There remain only you and Murry in our lives. We look at the others as across the grave. A death, and a grave lies between us and them. They are the other side of the grave, the old, far side, these —s and —s. We must not look back. There must be no looking back. There must be no more retrospection, which is introspection, no more remembering and interpreting. We must look forward into the unknown that is to be, like flowers that come up in the spring. Because we really *are* born again.

We have met one or two young people, just one or two, who have the germ of the new life in them. It doesn't matter what they are personally. Murry dismisses them with a sneer, for all that which is the *past* in them, but I hold on by that which is the future, which is gladdening.

We give up this flat tomorrow. For Christmas we go to my sister's in Derbyshire: c/o Mrs Clarke, Grosvenor Rd, Ripley, Derbyshire. We stay there till the 29th December. Then we go to the Beresfords' cottage in Cornwall, to live there till March. One or two others will come too. I want it now that we live together. When you come back, I want you and Murry to live with us, or near us, in unanimity; not these separations. Let us all live together and create a new world. If it is too difficult in England, because here all is destruction and dying and corruption, let us go away to Florida: soon. But let us go *together*, and keep together, several of us, as being of one spirit. Let it be a union in the unconsciousness, not in the consciousness. Get better soon, and come back, and let us all try to be happy *together*, in unanimity, not in hostility, creating, not destroying.

Love from me.

D. H. LAWRENCE

Ripley, Derbyshire.
Monday, 27 Dec., 1915

My dear Ottoline, –

Your letter and parcel came this morning. The books are splendid: but why did you give me the book, the Shelley, you must value it? It is gay and pretty. I shall keep it safe.

Did you like the Ajanta frescoes? I *loved* them: the pure fulfilment – the pure simplicity – the complete, almost perfect relations between the men and the women – the most perfect things I have *ever* seen. Botticelli is vulgar beside them. They are the zenith of a very lovely civilization, the crest of a very perfect wave of human development. I love them beyond everything pictorial that I have ever seen – the perfect, perfect intimate relation between the men and the women; so simple and complete, such a very perfection of passion, a fullness, a whole blossom. That which we call passion is a very one-sided thing, based chiefly on hatred and *Wille zur Macht*. There is no Will to Power here – it is so lovely – in those frescoes.

We are here in Ripley – suffering rather. It is a cruel thing to go back into the past; to turn our backs on the future and go back to that which one has been. I've just been differing violently with my eldest brother, who is a radical nonconformist.

Altogether the life here is so dark and violent; it all happens in the senses, powerful and rather destructive: no mind nor mental consciousness, unintellectual. These men are passionate enough, sensuous, dark – God, how all my boyhood comes back – so violent, so dark, the mind always dark and without understanding, the senses violently active. It makes me sad beyond words. These men, whom I love so much – and the life has such a power over me – they *understand* mentally so horribly: only industrialism, only wages and money and machinery. They can't *think* anything else. All their collective thinking is in those terms only. They are utterly unable to appreciate any pure, ulterior truth: only this industrial – mechanical – wage idea. This they will act from – nothing else. That is why we are *bound* to get something like Guild-Socialism in the long run, which is a reduction to the lowest terms – nothing higher than that which now is, only lower. But I suppose things have got to be reduced to their lowest terms. Only, oh God, I don't want to be implicated in it. It is necessary to get the germ of a new development *towards the highest*, not a reduction to the lowest. That we must do, in Cornwall and Florida; the germ of a new era. But here, the reduction to the lowest must go on.

The strange, dark, sensual life, so violent, and hopeless at the bottom, combined with this horrible paucity and material-ism of mental consciousness, makes me so sad, I could scream. They are still so living, so vulnerable, so darkly passionate. I love them like brothers – but, my God, I hate them too: I don't intend to own them as masters – not while the world stands. One must conquer them also – think beyond them, know beyond them, act beyond them.

But there will be a big row after the war, with these working men – I don't think I could bear to be here to see it. I couldn't bear it – this last reduction. But here they think the war will last long – they are not like London.

At last, at last, one will be able to set forth from it all, into the uncreated future, the unborn, unconceived era. One must leave all this to finish itself: the new unanimity, the new com-plete happiness beyond – one must be strong enough to create this.

Love from us both.

D. H. LAWRENCE

We go to Cornwall, on Thursday. There is the beginning.

Porthcothan, St Merryn,
Padstow, Cornwall.
7 Jan., 1916

MY DEAR KATHERINE, –

I hear Murry has gone to France to see you: good: also that you are well and happy: benissimo!

Give John my love.

I love being here in Cornwall – so peaceful, so far off from the world. But the world has disappeared for ever – there is no more world any more: only here, and a fine thin air which nobody and nothing pollutes.

My dear Katherine, I've done bothering about the world and people – I've finished. There now remains to find a nice place where one can be happy. And you and Jack will come if you like – when you feel like it: and we'll all be happy together – no more questioning and quibbling and trying to do anything with the world. The world is gone, extinguished, like the lights of last night's Café Royal – gone for ever. There is a new world with a new thin unsullied air and no people in it but new-born people: *moi-même et* Frieda.

No return to London and the world, my dear Katherine – it has disappeared, like the lights of last night's Café Royal.

We, Frieda and I, both send our love, for the New Year, the Year 1 of the new world. The same also to Murry. The old year had to die.

But I'm not going to struggle and strive with anything any more – go like a thistle-down, anywhere, having nothing to do with the world, no connexion.

Love to you.

D. H. LAWRENCE

Porthcothan, St Merryn,
Padstow, Cornwall.
1 *Feb.*, 1916

My dear Beresford, –

Thanks for your letter. We heard from Barbara Low that you think of coming back in February. Will you tell me, so that we can leave Emma a few days to make ready for you. I don't know where we shall go. It looks as if we shall have to go to a little place Lady Ottoline Morrell will lend us, for we are very badly off. But I should like to stay in Cornwall. I like it so much. We might afford a cottage, I think.

It is quite true what you say: the shore is absolutely primeval: those heavy, black rocks, like solid darkness, and the heavy water like a sort of first twilight breaking against them, and not changing them. It is really like the first craggy breaking of dawn in the world, a sense of the primeval darkness just behind, before the Creation. That is a very great and comforting thing to feel, I think: after all this whirlwind of dust and grit and dirty paper of a modern Europe. I love to see those terrifying rocks, like solid lumps of the original darkness, quite impregnable: and then the ponderous, cold light of the sea foaming up: it is marvellous. It is not sunlight. Sunlight is really fire-light. This cold light of the heavy sea is really the eternal light washing against the eternal darkness, a terrific abstraction, far beyond all life, which is merely of the sun, warm. And it does one's soul good to escape from the ugly triviality of life into this clash of two infinities one upon the other, cold and eternal.

The Cornish people still attract me. They have become detestable, I think, and yet they *aren't* detestable. They are, of course, strictly *anti-social* and un-Christian. But then, the aristocratic principle and the principle of magic, to which they belonged, these two have collapsed, and left only the most ugly, scaly, insect-like, unclean *selfishness*, so that each one of them is like an insect isolated within its own scaly, glassy envelope, and running seeking its own small end. And how foul that is! How they stink in their repulsiveness, in that way.

Nevertheless, the old race is still revealed, a race which believed in the darkness, in magic, and in the magic transcendency of one man over another, which is fascinating. Also there is left some of the old sensuousness of the darkness, a sort of softness, a sort of flowing together in physical intimacy, something almost negroid, which is fascinating.

But curse them, they are entirely mindless, and yet they are living purely for social advancement. They ought to be living in the darkness and warmth and passionateness of the blood, sudden, incalculable. Whereas they are like insects gone cold, living only for money, for *dirt*. They are foul in this. They ought all to die.

Not that I've seen very much of them – I've been laid up in bed. But going out, in the motor and so on, one sees them and feels them and knows what they are like.

Hawken was very cross because Heseltine, who is staying with me, chopped down a dead old tree in the garden. I said to him (Hawken), 'I'm sorry, but don't trouble. It was so dead it soon would have fallen. And you may take the wood.'

The young men are all being called now up round here. They are very miserable. There are loud lamentations on every hand. The only cry is, that they may not be sent out to France to fight. They all quite shamelessly don't want to *see* a gun. I sympathize perfectly with this.

The cursed war will go on for ever.

Don't let us keep you out of your house for one moment. If you want to come in in a week's time, only let us know, and all will be ready for you. We love the house and we love being here. But we can leave at a day's notice.

I have got ready a book of poetry here – quite ready – which I think is a great work to have done.

The Murrys write from France that they are *very* happy: for which I am very glad. They think of coming back in March.

My wife sends warmest greetings to Mrs Beresford and the child, and to you, in which I heartily join.

Yours,

D. H. LAWRENCE

41   TO J. M. MURRY AND KATHERINE MANSFIELD

Porthcothan, St Merryn,
N. Cornwall.
24th Feb., 1916

MY DEAR JACK AND KATHERINE, –

Now don't get in a state, you two, about nothing. The publishing scheme has not yet become at all real or important, to me.

Heseltine was mad to begin it – he wanted to get *The Rainbow* published. I felt, you don't know how much, sick and done. And it was rather fine that he believed and was so generously enthusiastic. He is the musical one: the musicians he likes are Delius, Goosens, Arnold Bax, and some few others. I believe as a matter of fact they are good, and we are perhaps, outside ourselves, more likely to have good music and bad books, than otherwise.

This is what is done, so far: a circular, or letter, something like that *Signature* one, only bigger and better, is drawn up, and 1000 copies are being printed. It is to be sent to everybody we can think of. Heseltine pays for all this.

It states that either there is a sufficient number of people to buy books, out of reverence for the books themselves, or else real books will disappear from us: therefore it is proposed to publish by subscription such works as are not likely to have any effect, coming through a publisher, or which are not likely to be published at all in the ordinary way: it is proposed to issue first *The Rainbow*, at 7/6 post-free. Will those who wish to partake in the scheme fill up the enclosed form. Then follows a form for subscription, just to be filled in, and re-addressed to Heseltine at his mother's house in Wales. I want to announce your book after *The Rainbow*.

He has gone to London, and I haven't yet seen a printed leaflet. When I get one I will send it you.

This is all. You see it is Heseltine's affair so far. I feel that he is one of those people who are transmitters, and not creators of art. And I don't think we are transmitters. I have come to the conclusion that I have no business genius. He is 21 years old, and I must say, I am very glad to have him for a friend. He lived here for seven weeks with us, so we know. Now don't think his friendship hurts ours. It doesn't touch it. You will like him too, because he is real, and has some queer kind of abstract passion which leaps into the future. He will be one with us. We must treasure and value very much anyone who will *really* be added on to us. I am afraid he may be conscripted.

And now, you two, for God's sake don't get in a state. I myself am always on the brink of another collapse. I begin to tremble and feel sick at the slightest upset: your letter for instance. Do be mild with me for a bit. Don't get silly notions. I've waited for you for two years now, and am far more constant to you than ever you are to me – or ever will be. Which you know. So don't use foolish language. I believe in you, and there's an end to it. But I think you keep far less faith with me than I with you, at the centre of things. But faith, like everything else, is a fluctuating thing. But that doesn't disprove its constancy. I know you will slip towards us again, however you may slip away and become nothing, or even go over to the enemy. It doesn't make any difference. You will in the main be constant to the same truth and the same spirit with me. The personal adherence, the me and thee business, is subsidiary to that. We are co-believers first. And in our oneness of belief lies our oneness. There is no *bond* anywhere. I am not bound to agree with you, nor you with me. We are not bound even to like each other: that is as it comes. But we gravitate to one belief, and that is our destiny, which is beyond choice. And in this destiny we are together.

This is my declaration, now let it be enough. As for this publishing business, the whole of the work remains yet to be done. We will fight together when you come. Meanwhile let Heseltine take the vanguard.

We went out looking for a house, and I think we have found one that is good. It is about 7 miles from St Ives, towards Land's End, very lonely, in the rocks on the sea, Zennor the nearest village: high pale hills, all moor-like and beautiful, behind very wild: 7 miles across country to Penzance: 25/– a week, eight rooms: a woman there who will clean for us.

We are going next Tuesday from here: address for the time being, 'The Tinner's Arms, Zennor, St Ives, Cornwall.' Or just Zennor: it is only seven houses to the church-tower: really beautiful. We take the house for four months, I think: March–June inclusive; with the option of staying on, I hope.

You will come at the end of April, when it will be warm. Just at present it is very cold. That icy wind you mention did not touch us at Fiascherino, but if we climbed up the hills, it was there: terrible. It has been blowing here also, and a bit of snow. Till now the weather has been so mild. Primroses and violets are out, and the gorse is lovely. At Zennor one sees infinite Atlantic, all peacock-mingled colours, and the gorse is sunshine itself, already. But this cold wind is deadly.

I have been in a sort of 'all gone but my cap' state this winter, and am very shaky. Also steering in my own direction with nobody to lend a hand or to come along, I feel very estranged. But when we set out to walk to Newquay, and when I looked down at Zennor, I knew it was the Promised Land, and that a new heaven and a new earth would take place. But everything is very tender in the bud, yet. But you will come along, in your own time, soon, I hope. You've escaped the worst of this winter. It has been the worst: one has touched the bottom. Somehow I have a sense of a new spring coming very joyful from the unknown.

My love to you both.　　　　　D. H. LAWRENCE

We shall be very badly off soon – and no incomings anywhere. I don't know what we shall do. But I don't bother. It will turn out somehow. Do let the winter be gone, before Katherine comes to England.

Tinner's Arms, Zennor,
St Ives, Cornwall.
8 *March,* 1916

My dear Jack and Katherine, –

We have taken our little cottage for £5 a year and are getting ready to furnish. Of course we shall want *very* little, having the things left from Byron Villas.

Really, you must have the other place. I keep looking at it. I call it already Katherine's house, Katherine's tower. There is something *very* attractive about it. It is very old, native to the earth, like rock, yet dry and all in the light of the hills and the sea. It is only twelve strides from our house to yours: we can talk from the windows: and besides us, only the gorse, and the fields, the lambs skipping and hopping like anything, and seagulls fighting with the ravens, and sometimes a fox, and a ship on the sea.

You must come, and we will live there a long, long time, very cheaply. You see, we must live somewhere, and it is so free and beautiful, and it will cost us so very little.

And don't talk any more of treacheries and so on. Henceforward let us take each other on trust – I'm sure we can. We are so few, and the world is so many, it is absurd that we are scattered. Let us be really happy and industrious together.

I don't know yet what will happen to Heseltine, whether he will be exempted. But I hope you will really like him, and we can all be friends together. He is the only one we can all be friends with.

But if you don't want him to have a room in your house – of course he would share expenses – he could have one elsewhere. Of course he may be kept away indefinitely.

But at any rate, you two come, and we shall be four together. It is cheaper to furnish a little, and pay £16 a year rent, than to pay £75 a year for a furnished place. And I'm sure we can live happily at Tregerthen: Tregerthen, Zennor, St Ives.

It is still cold. Snow falls sometimes, then vanishes at once. When the sun shines, some gorse bushes smell hot and sweet. Flocks of birds are flying by, to go to the Scilly Isles to nest, and the blackbirds sing in the chill evenings. We got big bunches of wallflowers in Penzance for a penny – we saw a man plucking them in a field – and they smell very good. But the wind still blows storms with snow out of the sea.

I heard from — still in the Pity-me sort of voice. He lies in the mud and murmurs about his dream-soul, and says that *action* is irrelevant. Meanwhile he earns diligently in munitions.

Do you think the war will end this year?

Much love from us both.

D. H. LAWRENCE

I suppose you have got my Monday's letter telling you all about the house. Your place has seven rooms: kitchen, dining-room, study, and upstairs, tower-room and 3 bedrooms. It was 3 old cottages.

Your letter of the 4th has just come – Thursday. Good, all is well between us all. No more quarrels and quibbles. Let it be agreed for ever. I am *Blutbruder: a Blutbrüderschaft* between us all. Tell K. *not* to be so queasy. Won't Farbman stick to your house? Much love from us both to you two. – D. H. L.

43   TO LADY CYNTHIA ASQUITH

Higher Tregerthen, Zennor,
St Ives, Cornwall.
Wednesday, April 26th, 1916

MY DEAR LADY CYNTHIA, –

It seems as if we were all going to be dragged into the *danse macabre*. One can only grin, and be fatalistic. My dear nation is bitten by the tarantula, and the venom has gone home at last. Now it is dance, *mes amis*, to the sound of the knuckle-bones.

It is very sad, but one isn't sad any more. It is done now, and no use crying over spilt milk. 'Addio' to everything. The poor dear old ship of Christian democracy is scuttled at last, the breach is made, the veil of the temple is torn, our epoch is over. *Soit!* I don't care, it's not my doing, and I can't help it. It isn't a question of 'dancing while Rome burns', as you said to me on the omnibus that Sunday evening – do you remember? It is a question of bobbing about gaily in chaos. 'Carpe diem' is the motto now: pure gay fatalism. It makes me laugh. My good old moral soul is *crevé.*

Will you tell me, if you can, what it would be wisest for me to do, at this juncture? Ought one to attest, and if so, what sort of job can I do? I don't *want* to do anything; but what will be, will be, and I haven't any conscience in the matter. If I have to serve, all right: only I should like a job that was at least sufferable. Do think a little, and advise me: or ask Herbert Asquith to tell me what I could do. I think it is all rather ridiculous – even when it is a question of life and death; such a scurry and a scuffle and a meaningless confusion that it is only a farce.

It is very lovely down here, the slopes of desert dead grass and heather sheering down to a sea that is so big and blue. I don't want a bit to have to go away. But it will keep. And the cottage is *very nice,* so small and neat and lovely. There is one next door, the same as this, that you must have when the pot bubbles too hard out there in the world. Will you be coming this way, when you are making your round of visits?

I am still waiting for my book of *Italian Sketches* to appear. Now there is a strike among the printers in Edinburgh. But it won't be long. It is quite a nice book. I will send you a copy.

I am doing another novel – that really occupies me. The world crackles and bursts, but that is another matter, external, in chaos. One has a certain order inviolable in one's soul. There one sits, as in a crow's nest, out of it all. And even if one is conscripted, still I can sit in my crow's nest of a soul and grin. Life mustn't be taken seriously any more, at least, the outer, social life. The social being I am has become a spectator at a knockabout dangerous farce. The individual particular me remains self-contained and grins. But I should be mortally indignant if I lost my life or even too much of my liberty, by being dragged into the knockabout farce of this social life.

I hope we shall see you soon. We might have some good times together – real good times, not a bit macabre, but jolly and full. The macabre touch bores me excessively.

Frieda is boiling the washing in a saucepan. I am, for the moment, making a portrait of Taimur-i-lang – Tamerlane, the Tartar: copying it from a 15th-century Indian picture. I like it very much.

Mila salute di cuore.

D. H. Lawrence

44   To Catherine Carswell

Higher Tregerthen, Zennor,
St Ives, Cornwall.
9th July, 1916

My dear Catherine, –

I never wrote to tell you that they gave me a complete exemption from all military service, thanks be to God. That was a week ago last Thursday. I had to join the Colours in Penzance, be conveyed to Bodmin (60 miles), spend a night in barracks with all the other men, and then be examined. It was experience enough for me, of soldiering. I am sure I should die in a week, if they kept me. It is the annulling of all one stands for, this militarism, the nipping of the very germ of one's being. I was very much upset. The sense of spiritual disaster everywhere was quite terrifying. One was not sure whether one survived or not. Things are very bad.

Yet I liked the men. They all seemed so *decent*. And yet they all seemed as if they had *chosen wrong*. It was the underlying sense of disaster that overwhelmed me. They are all so brave, to suffer, but none of them brave enough, to reject suffering. They are all so noble, to accept sorrow and hurt, but they can none of them demand happiness. Their manliness all lies in accepting calmly this death, this loss of their integrity. They must stand by their fellow man: that is the motto.

This is what Christ's weeping over Jerusalem has brought

us to, a whole Jerusalem offering itself to the Cross. To me, this is infinitely more terrifying than Pharisees and Publicans and Sinners, taking *their* way to death. This is what the love of our neighbour has brought us to, that, because one man dies, we all die.

This is the most terrible madness. And the worst of it all, is, that it is a madness of righteousness. These Cornish are most, most unwarlike, soft, peaceable, ancient. No men could suffer more than they, at being conscripted – at any rate, those that were with me. Yet they accepted it all: they accepted it, as one of them said to me, with wonderful purity of spirit – I could howl my eyes out over him – because 'they believed first of all in their duty to their fellow man'. There is no falsity about it: they believe in their duty to their fellow man. And what duty is this, which makes us forfeit everything, because Germany invaded Belgium? Is there nothing beyond my fellow man? If not, then there is nothing beyond myself, beyond my own throat, which may be cut, and my own purse, which may be slit: because *I* am the fellow man of all the world, my neighbour is but myself in a mirror. So we toil in a circle of pure egoism.

This is what 'love thy neighbour as thyself' comes to. It needs only a little convulsion, to break the mirror, to turn over the coin, and there I have myself, my own purse, I, I, I, we, we, we – like the newspapers today: 'Capture the trade – unite the Empire – *à bas les autres*.'

There needs something else besides the love of the neighbour. If all my neighbours chose to go down the slope to Hell, that is no reason why I should go with them. I know in my own soul a truth, a right, and no amount of neighbours can weight it out of the balance. I know that, for me, the war is wrong. I know that if the Germans wanted my little house, I would rather give it them than fight for it: because my little house is not important enough to me. If another man must fight for his house, the more's the pity. But it is his affair. To fight for possessions, goods, is what my soul *will not* do. Therefore it will not fight for the neighbour who fights for his own goods.

All this war, this talk of nationality, to me is false. I *feel* no nationality, not fundamentally. I feel no passion for my own land, nor my own house, nor my own furniture, nor my own money. Therefore I won't pretend any. Neither will I take part in the scrimmage, to help my neighbour. It is his affair to go in or to stay out, as he wishes.

If they had compelled me to go in, I should have died, I am sure. One is too raw, one fights too hard already, for the real integrity of one's being. That last straw of compulsion would have been too much, I think.

Christianity is based on the love of self, the love of property, one degree removed. Why should I care for my neighbour's property, or my neighbour's life, if I do not care for my own? If the truth of my spirit is all that matters to me, in the last issue, then on behalf of my neighbour, all I care for is the truth of *his* spirit. And if his truth is his love of property, I refuse to stand by him, whether he be a poor man robbed of his cottage, his wife and children, or a rich man robbed of his merchandise. I have nothing to do with him, in that wise, and I don't care whether he keep or lose his throat, on behalf of his property. Property, and power – which is the same – is *not* the criterion. The criterion is the truth of my own intrinsic desire, clear of ulterior contamination.

I hope you aren't bored. Something makes me state my position, when I write to you.

It is summer, but not very summery, such heavy rain. I told you the Murrys had gone away, to south Cornwall. Now she doesn't like that. I believe she is in London at present. She is very dissatisfied with him.

We are keeping on their house for the rest of their year. It is *so* near, that if strangers came, it would be intolerable. So I am buying a very little furniture – it is so cheap and *so* nice here, second-hand – to furnish a sitting-room and a bedroom, for the visitors. I think Dollie Radford is coming in about a week's time, then Barbara Low. We get such pleasure, looking at old tables and old chairs: a big round rose-wood table, very large, 4 ft 4 ins. diameter and solid, 10/–: three very nice birch-wood chairs, 7/6d.: an armchair, 5/–: the sitting-room is furnished: it is an upper room, with big windows, and shelves.

It is such a pleasure, buying this furniture – I remember my sermon. But one doesn't really care. This cottage, that I like so much – and the new table, and the chairs – I could leave them all tomorrow, blithely. Meanwhile, they are very nice.

I have finished my novel, and am going to try to type it. It will be a labour – but we have got no money. But I am asking Pinker for some. And if it bores me to type the novel, I shan't do it. There is a last chapter to write, some time, when one's heart is not so contracted.

I think you are not very wise to go to the Hebrides with Carswell's people – you would be so much happier with him alone – or with friends.

Greiffenhagen seems to be slipping back and back. I suppose it has to be. Let the dead bury their dead. Let the past smoulder out. One shouldn't look back, like Lot's wife: though why *salt*, that I could never understand.

Have you got a copy of *Twilight in Italy*? If not, I have got one to give you. So just send me word, a p.c.

Frieda sends many greetings.

Yours,

D. H. LAWRENCE

I am amused to hear of Carswell's *divorce* case.

---

45 TO J. M. MURRY

Higher Tregerthen, Zennor,
St Ives, Cornwall.
28 Aug., 1916

DEAR JACK, –

Thank you very much for your book on Dostoievsky, which has just come. I have only just looked in it here and there – and read the epilogue. I wonder how much you or anybody else is ready to face out the old life, and so transcend it. An epoch of the human mind may have come to the end in Dostoievsky: but humanity is capable of going on a very long way further yet, in a state of mindlessness – curse it. And you've got the cart before the horse. <u>It isn't the being that must follow the mind, but the mind must follow the being.</u> And if only the cursed cowardly world had the courage to follow its own being with its mind, if it only had the courage to know what its unknown *is*, its own desires and its own activities, it might get beyond to the new secret. But the trick is, when you draw somewhere near the 'brink of the revelation', to dig your head in the sand like the disgusting ostrich, and see the revelation there. Meanwhile, with their head in the sand of pleasing visions and secrets and revelations, they kick and squirm with their behinds, most disgustingly. I don't blame humanity for having no mind, I blame it for putting its mind in a box and using it as a nice little self-gratifying instrument. You've got to know, and know everything, before you 'transcend' into the 'unknown'. But Dostoievsky, like the rest, can nicely stick his head between the feet of Christ, and waggle his behind in the air. And though the behind-wagglings are a revelation, I don't think much even of the feet of Christ as a bluff for the cowards to hide their eyes against.

You want to be left alone – so do I – by everybody, by the whole world, which is despicable and contemptible to me and sickening.

D. H. LAWRENCE

46 TO MRS T. D. D.

Higher Tregerthen, Zennor,
St Ives, Cornwall.
31 *Oct.*, 1916

MY DEAR MRS D., –
I was glad to have your card from Leghorn, telling us you were joyfully in Italy again with D. I wonder where you are now – back again in Milan? – and enjoying everything, I hope.

What about the children? – though for my part, I think husbands and wives more important than children, so long as the latter are well looked after.

Here we are, still sitting lonelily over the sea like a couple of motionless cormorants. I have just finished a novel, which everybody will hate *completely*. But if I can only get a little money for it, I shall come to Italy. My health is miserable, damnable. I seem half my time, and more, to be laid up in bed. I think the terrible moisture of England does it: it has rained every day now for nine weeks. I think in Italy I should be better. So I shall try to come. What do you think?

I should not go back to Fiascherino – I couldn't bear it. It is always lacerating to go back to the past: and then to find our beloved old Felice more old, and unhappy for the death of poor Elide – no, I couldn't stand it, I should be a fountain of tears. I should like to go to Rome. I don't know why, but one seems drawn to the great historic past, now the present had become so lamentably historic. So I want to go to Rome, and see if I should be better and happier there. Then we should spend a day or two in Milan *en passant*, to see you and D. again: which would be a *great* pleasure.

I don't know that there is any news that I can tell you. — is expecting an infant: everybody says 'poor infant'. But — is happy and important at last. I think she feels no woman ever had a child before, and she is the inventress of the human race: which no doubt is quite the right spirit.

Of ourselves there is no news. Barring poverty and a few jolts, we are very happy together. Frieda is allowed interviews with her children occasionally: which makes things easier. I, you will not forget, have a beard: purplish red, people say. I must keep you reminded so you should not be shocked, when we arrive in Milan. How do you find Italy? Still pretty nonchalant and happy in itself, I hope. I should hate to come to a tragic country.

D. very nobly offered to lend me money: which, for some reason, scared me. I should feel a monster, taking money from a man with a wife and three children, and only his salary to keep them on. No, when I am forced to beg for a penny to throw between the teeth of the wolf at the door, I shall ask rich people for it: they will give it me: I don't let myself be worried.

I shall address this letter to D., so that if you are come back to England he will read it and write to me.

Do you like Milan? I didn't. But I've got a longing to go to Rome.

All good greetings from Frieda and me to both.

Yours,

D. H. Lawrence

47   To Lady Cynthia Asquith

Zennor, St Ives, Cornwall.
Monday, 11th December, 1916

Here's a pretty state of affairs – Messrs Lloyd George and Lord Derby – funny – pretty! This is the last stage of all, that ends our sad eventful history. So be it.

Over Cornwall, last Wednesday and Thursday, went a terrible wave of depression. In Penzance market, farmers went about with wonderstruck faces, saying, 'We're beaten. I'm afraid we're beaten. These Germans are a wonderful nation, I'm afraid. They are more than a match for us.' That is Cornwall at the present time. I must say, I too expect a national disaster before very long, but I don't care very much. They want it, the people in this country. They want in their vile underneath way of working to scuttle the old ship and pitch everybody into water. Well, let them. Perhaps when we've all had a ducking in the sea of fearful disaster, we shall be more wholesome and truthful. At any rate, then I feel we shall be able to do something, something new. It is no use adhering to that old advanced crowd – Cambridge, Lowes Dickenson, Bertie Russell, young reformers, Socialists, Fabians – they are our disease, not our hope. We want a clean sweep, and a new start, and we will have it. Wait only a little longer. Fusty, fuzzy peace-cranks and lovers of humanity are the devil. We must get on a new track altogether. Damn Humanity, let me have a bit of inhuman, or non-human truth, that our fuzzy human emotions can't alter.

I send you MS. of a tiny book of poems, to see if you like them. If you do, and if they find a publisher, I think they might be a real success – and I would like to inscribe them to you – 'To Cynthia Asquith'. Damn initials. But that is just as you like.

We keep putting off our coming to London, but it is bound to be within a month's time now – probably in early January. Then we must see where we are, how we stand, all of us. What we feel and what we are ready for.

D. H. LAWRENCE

The story 'The Thimble' is being published in an American magazine called *The Seven Arts*.

48   TO CATHERINE CARSWELL

Zennor, St Ives,
Cornwall.
Monday, 5th January, 1917

MY DEAR CATHERINE, –
I never answered your last letter. We seem all to be pretty downed, floored. I feel myself awfully like a fox that is cornered by a pack of hounds and boors who don't perhaps know he's there, but are closing in unconsciously. It seems to me to be a crucial situation now: whether we are nabbed by the old vile world, and destroyed, or whether we manage, with the help of the unseen, to make good our escape. I am applying for reindorsement of my passports to New York. If I can but get it done, and if no other horror, like American exclusion, intervenes, I shall be off at once: this month, I hope. I feel it is really a question of to be or not to be. If we are to be, then we must move at once out of this into another world. Otherwise it is not to be.

My dear Catherine, for me the hour is crucial. But every thing has its season. Perhaps your times are a little different. Perhaps – this in answer to your last letter – it is necessary for you and Don to have another bout, another round, to try another fall with this old world. Every man has his own times and his own destiny apart and single. It only remains for us to fulfil that which is *really* in us. For me, it is time to go:

> 'Time for us to go,
> Time for us to go . . .'

as the song is.

I don't know why I go to America – except that I feel all right in going there. One instinctively takes one's way, and it is all right. I feel we shall get off. I am not beaten yet. But don't say anything about our going, will you?

Everybody refuses to publish the novel. It will not get done over here. I don't care.

As a sort of last work, I have gathered and shaped my last poems into a book. It is a sort of final conclusion of the old life in me – 'and now farewell', is really the motto. I don't much want to submit the MS. for publication. It is very intimate and vital to me. But I have got it *very nearly* ready. Would you like to see it? I will send it you if you would.

How is Joanna? My heart aches a bit for her: it is so wintry for her to come forth. Have patience and courage. *Write for America* if you can't write. I find I am unable to write for England any more – the response has gone quite dead and dumb. A certain hope rises in my heart, quite hot, and I can go on. But it is not England. It seems to me it is America. If I am kept here I am beaten for ever.

How are you yourself, and Don? The weeks go by very bitterly, don't you find? They are hardly bearable.

The weather is cold down here also: but sometimes very sunny, as today. We live on tenterhooks, hoping for departure. You too will move away, when your time comes.

Do you see Esther Andrews? And how is she? We want her to go with us to America, and to the ultimate place we call Typee or Rananim. There is indeed such an ultimate place.

Don't treat me as I have treated you, and make me wait a long time for an answer. Write soon.

D. H. LAWRENCE

Zennor, St Ives,
Cornwall.
12th February, 1917

They have refused to endorse my passport. It is a bitter blow, because I must go to America. But I will try again in a little time.

How are you, and what are you doing? For me the skies have fallen, here in England, and there is an end. I must go to America as soon as I can, because to remain here now, after the end, is like remaining on one's death-bed. It is necessary to begin a new life.

You mustn't think I haven't cared about England. I have cared deeply and bitterly. But something is broken. There *is not* any England. One must look now for another world. This is only a tomb.

I must wait, and try again in a little time. I don't want to bother you with woes or troubles. Only I feel there is some sort of connexion between our fates – yours and your children's and your husband's, and Frieda's and mine. I know that sometime or other I shall pull through. And then, when I can help you or your husband or the children, that will be well. Because, don't hide away the knowledge, real life is finished here, it is over. The skies have already fallen. There are no heavens above us, no hope. It needs a beginning elsewhere. That will be more true, perhaps, of Herbert Asquith and of John the Son, than of you. But it is a bit of knowledge not to be evaded even while one struggles through with the present.

I feel the War won't be so very much longer. The skies have *really* fallen. There is no need of any more pulling at the pillars.

New earth, new heaven, that is what one must find. I don't think America is a new world. But there is a living sky above. America I know is shocking. But there is a new sky above it. I must go to America as soon as ever I can. Do you think I don't know what it is to be an Englishman? . . .

There is no news here, we seem as in a lost world. My health is fair. It is the old collapsing misery that kills one. Frieda sends her love.

D. H. LAWRENCE

50   TO LADY CYNTHIA ASQUITH

Hermitage, Berks.
Thursday, April, 1917

MY DEAR LADY CYNTHIA, –

I didn't ring you up, because on Sunday, suddenly, I collapsed with sickness, and was quite seedy. Then just as suddenly on Tuesday, my soul inspired itself and I got well. So, yesterday I came on here. Tomorrow I am going back to Cornwall, thank God.

It was the evil influence of aggregate London that made me ill: suddenly I start to be sick. It is all very vile.

It is much best for you to go down to Stanway. The spring is here, the cuckoo is heard, primroses and daffodils are out in the woods, it is very lovely. I feel that the buds as they unfold, and the primroses come out, are really stronger than all the armies and all the War. I feel as if the young grass growing would upset all the cannon on the face of the earth, and that man with his evil stupidity is after all nothing, the leaves just brush him aside. The principle of life is after all stronger than the principle of death, and I spit on your London and your government and your armies.

Come and see us whenever you are near enough and feel like it. The state of your desperation is really a thing to be ashamed of. It all comes of submitting and acquiescing in things one *does not vitally believe in.* If you learned flatly to reject things which are false to you, you wouldn't sell yourself to such deadness. One should stick by one's own soul, and by nothing else. In one's soul, one knows the truth from the untruth, and life from death. And if one betrays one's own soul-knowledge one is the worst of traitors. I am out of all patience with the submitting to the things that be, however foul they are, just because they happen to be. But there will fall a big fire on the city before long, as on Sodom and Gomorrah, and will burn us clean of a few politicians, etc., and of some of our own flunkeying to mere current baseness. I feel angry with you, the way you have betrayed everything that is real, by admitting the superiority of that which is merely temporal and foul and external upon us. If all the aristocrats have sold the vital principle of life to the mere current of foul affairs, what good are the aristocrats? As for the people, they will serve to make a real bust-up, quite purposeless and aimless. But when the bust-up is made and the place more or less destroyed we can have a new start.

It is a very lovely day. Hope you are well.

D. H. LAWRENCE

51   To CATHERINE CARSWELL

Zennor, St Ives, Cornwall.
11th May, 1917

MY DEAR CATHERINE, —

There isn't any news, either about the *Reality of Peace* or anything else. Only Esther Andrews has gone back to London, so I expect you will be seeing her soon.

We are having very beautiful weather, so hot and bright. I have never seen anything so beautiful as the gorse this year, and the blackthorn. The gorse blazes in sheets of yellow fire, and the blackthorn is like white smoke, filling the valley bed. Primroses and violets are full out, and the bluebells are just coming. It is very magnificent and royal. The sun is just sinking in a flood of gold. One would not be astonished to see the cherubim flashing their wings and coming towards us, from the west. All the time, one seems to be expecting an arrival from the beyond, from the heavenly world. The sense of something, someone magnificent approaching, is so strong, it is a wonder one does not see visions in the heavens.

I was glad to hear that the novel was going. When it is done, you will send it me, won't you? It will be really something overcome, a phase surpassed in you, when the book is finished.

I am not doing anything, except garden, just now. Yesterday I began to type out the *Peace* articles – I want another copy – and I was recasting the second one. But suddenly I felt as if I was going dotty, straight out of my mind, so I left off. One can only wait and let the crisis come and go.

My gardens are so lovely, everything growing in rows, and so fast – such nice green rows of all kinds of young things. It looks like a triumph of life in itself. But these need rain, we are very dry on these slopes.

Frieda is much better in health these last two days. She sends her love. I hope the eggs won't get broken. Send the box back, and you can have some more. I'm glad Don is all right. I'm sure the war will end soon. I wonder if I *am* a bit dotty.

D. H. Lawrence

No news yet of the desk. Please send me the bill for packing – you are poor now.

52   To Edward Marsh

*Zennor, St Ives,
Cornwall.*

26 June, 1917

Dear Eddie, –

Thank you very much for the cheque for £7. 15s. It is a nice sum, and *Georgian Poetry* is a good goose, her egg is much appreciated, and I hope she will live for ever.

I got myself rejected again at Bodmin on Saturday: cursed the loathsome performance. As for flourishing, I should like to flourish a pistol under the nose of the fools that govern us. They make one spit with disgust. Only let the skies break, and we will flourish on top of the 'times', and the time-keepers and the time-servers.

Yrs,
D. H. LAWRENCE

53   TO LADY CYNTHIA ASQUITH

Zennor, St Ives,
Cornwall.

12th October, 1917

MY DEAR LADY CYNTHIA, –

Now comes another nasty blow. The police have suddenly descended on the house, searched it, and delivered us a notice to leave the area of Cornwall, by Monday next. So on Monday we shall be in London, staying, if possible c/o Mrs Radford, 32, Well Walk, Hampstead, N.W.

This bolt from the blue has fallen this morning: why, I know not, any more than you do. I cannot even conceive how I have incurred suspicion – have not the faintest notion. We are as innocent even of pacifist activities, let alone spying of any sort as the rabbits in the field outside. And we must leave Cornwall, and live in an unprohibited area, and report to the police. It is *very* vile. We have practically no money at all – I don't know what we shall do.

At any rate we shall be in London Monday evening. You can see us if you feel like it during the week.

This order comes from W. Western, Major-General i/c Administration, Southern Command, Salisbury. They have taken away some of my papers – I don't know what. It is all very sickening, and makes me very weary.

I hope things are all right with you.

D. H. LAWRENCE

44, *Mecklenburgh Square, W.C.1.*
Wednesday

You are only half right about the disciples and the alabaster box. If Jesus had paid more attention to Magdalene, and less to his disciples, it would have been better. It was not the ointment-pouring which was so devastating, but the discipleship of the twelve.

As for me and my 'women', I know what they are and aren't, and though there is a certain messiness, there is a further reality. Take away the subservience and feet-washing, and the pure understanding between the Magdalene and Jesus went deeper than the understanding between the disciples and Jesus, or Jesus and the Bethany women. But Jesus himself was frightened of the knowledge which subsisted between the Magdalene and him, a knowledge deeper than the knowledge of Christianity and 'good', deeper than love, anyhow.

And both you and Frieda need to go one world deeper in knowledge. As for spikenard, if I chance to luxuriate in it, it is by the way: not so very Philippically filthy either. Not that it matters.

I don't mind a bit being told where I am wrong – not by you or anybody I respect. Only you don't seem to be going for me in anything where I am really wrong: a bit Pharisaic, both you and Frieda: external.

It seems to me there is a whole world of knowledge to forsake, a new, deeper, lower one to *entamer*. And your hatred of me, like Frieda's hatred of me, is your cleavage to a world of knowledge and being which you ought to forsake, which, by organic law, you must depart from or die. And my 'women' represent, in an impure and unproud, subservient, cringing, bad fashion, I admit – but represent none the less the threshold of a new world, or underworld, of knowledge and being. And the Hebridean songs, which represent you and Frieda in this, are songs of the damned: that is, songs of those who inhabit an underworld which is forever an underworld, never to be made open and whole. And you would like us all to inhabit a suggestive underworld which is never revealed or opened, only intimated, only *felt* between the initiated. — I won't have it. The old world must burst, the underworld must be open and whole, new world. You want an emotional sensuous underworld, like Frieda and the Hebrideans: my 'women' want an ecstatic subtly-intellectual underworld, like the Greeks — Orphicism — like Magdalene at her feet-washing — and there you are.

D. H. LAWRENCE

55   To CECIL GRAY

Chapel Farm Cottage, Hermitage,
Nr Newbury, Berks.
12 *March,* 1918

How are you finding Bosigran? — if you have got back there. I hope it is nice, now the weather is soft and sunny. I wrote to Capt. Short to say I wouldn't keep on the cottages at Tregerthen — also I wrote to William Henry, to tell him the same news. But I have not yet quite decided what to do about the furniture. My sister gets furious if I say we may not go near her. Yet she does not find us a house. On the other hand, there are two charming cottages here — one down in a little village, fast asleep for ever: a cottage just under the hill, under the hazel-woods, with its little garden backing to the old churchyard, where the sunny, grey, square-towered church dozes on without rousing: the other on the hill touching the wood. Frieda of course is *dying* for one of these. And when we were down in Hampstead Norris yesterday, I quite shook with panic, lest we should actually go and take the cottage under the hill by the church. A real panic comes over me, when I feel I am on the brink of taking another house. I truly wish I were a fox or a bird — but my ideal now is to have a caravan and a horse, and move on for ever, and never have a neighbour. This is a real after-the-war ideal. There is a gipsy camp near here – and how I envy them – down a sandy lane under some pine trees.

I find here one is soothed with trees. I never knew how soothing trees are – many trees, and patches of open sunlight, and tree-presences – it is almost like having another being. At the moment the thought of the sea makes me verily shudder.

I ebb along with the American essays, which are in their last and final form. In them, I have got it all off my chest. I shall never write another page of philosophy – or whatever it is – when these are done. Thank God for that. Yet it is absolutely necessary to get it out, fix it, and have a definite foothold, to be *sure*. Of course I think the world ought to hold up its hands in marvelling thankfulness for such profound and relieving exposition. And of course I see the world doing it.

It is very spring-like. In spite of the fact that I *think* the war will last for ever, I believe this particular war with Germany won't last so very much longer, on our part. Not that it matters; all the world – people won't alter: and they won't die in sufficient quantities to matter. I have come to think that it is enough to lapse along pleasantly with the days. It is very nice. That is why the cottage in the village fills me with such panic. I believe I could go into a soft sort of Hardy-sleep, hearing the church chime from hour to hour, watching the horses at the farm drink at the pond, writing pages that *seemed* beautifully important, and having visits from people who *seemed* all wrong, as coming from the inferior outer world.

But no doubt some new sword of Damocles is just spinning to drop on one's head.

I don't know why you and I don't get on very well when we are together. But it seems we don't. It seems we are best apart. You seem to go winding on in some sort of process that just winds me in the other direction. You might just tell me when you think your process is ended, and we'll look at each other again. Meanwhile you dance on in some sort of sensuous dervish dance that winds my brain up like a ticking bomb. God save us, what a business it is even to be acquainted with another creature. But I suppose one day we might hit it off. Be quick and wind yourself to the end. The one thing I don't seem to be able to stand is the presence of anybody else – barring Frieda, sometimes. Perhaps I shall get over it.

I shall ask you if I want any help at Tregerthen, in the removing. Meanwhile adieu. Frieda greets you.

D. H. LAWRENCE

But I do loathe possessing things, and having another house. If only one could be an animal, with a thick warm hide, and never a stitch or rag besides. <u>Nobody ought to own houses or furniture – any more than they own the stones of the high-road.</u>

56   TO CECIL GRAY

Chapel Farm Cottage, Hermitage,
Nr Newbury, Berks.

18 *April,* 1918

MY DEAR GRIGIO, –

I was up in the Midlands for a week last week – my sister negotiating for a little place for us – a bungalow on the brow of the steep valley at Via Gellia – near Cromford. We should have it furnished, for a year – my sister would pay for it – if the people agree to let. It is a nice place – with pleasant little grounds, and two rough fields. We should hear in a day or two about it. And then, if the people let it us, we shall go in a week or ten days' time. It is quite open and free – you would have to come and see us there.

Frieda went to London and saw her children and it all went off quite pleasantly and simply, apparently. I feel unsettled here now, as if we must move soon. And we *must* move – the Radfords want to come here in May.

I have made a little book of poems that Beaumont asked me for – all smallish, lyrical pieces. I have been doing poetry for a few weeks now – I want to make a second little book. But it is exhausting to keep it up. The first book has 18 poems, it more or less refers to the war, and is called *Bay*. I don't know if Beaumont will really do it. The second would be different – I would call it *Chorus of Women*, or something like that.

That's all the news – except that yesterday there was deep snow, though the trees are in bloom. Plum trees and cherry trees full of blossom look so queer in a snow landscape, their lovely foamy fullness goes a sort of pinky drab, and the snow looks fiendish in its cold incandescence. I hated it violently.

I hope we shan't be bothered by the military. I believe as a matter of fact they have too bad an opinion of us – let us hope so. I don't believe, moreover, that they will have the *energy* to comb out all those things that stick at all tight. There is a great exhaustedness coming.

Richard* sent me a line to say he was off to France. I believe he was glad to go. It is harder to bear the pressure of the vacuum over here than the stress of congestion over there.

I am reading Gibbon. I am quite happy with those old Roman emperors – they were so out-and-out, they just did as they liked, and *vogue la galère*, till they were strangled. I can do with them. I also read two ponderous tomes on Africa, by a German called Frobenius. He says there was a great West African – Zomban (?) – civilization, which preceded Egypt and Carthage, and gave rise to the Atlantis myth. But he is a tiresome writer.

Let us hear from you.

D. H. L.

57   To Lady Cynthia Asquith

Mountain Cottage,
        Middleton-by-Wirksworth, Derby.
                        3rd June, 1918

I dreamed of you so hard a few days ago, so must write, though there is no news to send. We are here with my sister,
*Aldington

and two children – a very delightful boy of three, and a girl of seven. I am surprised how children are like barometers to their parents' feelings. There is some sort of queer, magnetic, psychic connexion – something a bit fatal, I believe. I feel I am all the time rescuing my nephew and my niece from their respective mothers, my two sisters; who have jaguars of wrath in their souls, however they purr to their offspring. The phenomenon of motherhood, in these days, is a strange and rather frightening phenomenon.

I dreamed, also, such a funny dream. When I had been to some big, crowded fair somewhere – where things were to sell, on booths and on the floor – as I was coming back down an open road, I heard such a strange crying overhead, in front, and looking up, I saw, not very high in the air above me, but higher than I could throw, two pale spotted dogs, crouching in the air, and mauling a bird that was crying loudly. I ran fast forwards and clapped my hands and the dogs started back. The bird came falling to earth. It was a young peacock, blue all over like a peacock's neck, very lovely. It still kept crying. But it was not much hurt. A woman came running out of a cottage not far off, and took the bird, saying it would be all right. So I went my way.

That dream is in some oblique way or other connected with your 'Aura' – but I can't interpret it.

Would you really like to come here – it's a nice place really – you'd like it. But I feel as if I were on a sort of ledge half-way down a precipice, and did not know how to get up or down; and it is a queer kind of place to ask visitors to see you, such a ledge.

I signed the agreement for the poems. When proofs come I'll send them to you and you can tell me at once if there is anything you'd like different. But they're all right.

Poor Whibley, he is so good trying to get that money for me. Will it come off? I hope so – but if not, never bother.

D. H. L.

Mountain Cottage,
Middleton-by-Wirksworth, Derby.
Sunday 1 Sept., 1918

Dear Don, –

We got home quite nicely last evening – but a terrible crush in the train from Gloucester to Derby. It seems very quiet here – strangely quiet, though the rain* blusters and the rain beats on this little house.

We were very happy with you, after the malaise of the first tumbling into that forest of Lydbrook – which for some reason is curiously upsetting. You were both awfully nice to us – it leaves a warm feeling. I hope you will be able to come here. I loved the walk to Simmond's Yat – particularly through that parky place – also the Monmouth day – particularly the church by the Monnow bridge – the bright sunny town, and the tears in one's inside because there isn't *real* peace – and then, *very nice*, the meal in the green riding: also our evenings. – They are good memories – worth a lot really. And it pleases me that we carried the child about. One has the future in one's arms, so to speak: and one *is* the present.

If you would care to, I wish you would read the essays I left with Catherine. You will say I repeat myself – that I don't know the terms of real philosophy – and that my terms are empty – the empty self – so don't *write* these things to me, I know them beforehand, and they make me cross. None the less, read the essays and see if you find anything in them.

I imagine you in that vicarage room this evening – no more 'What are the wild waves saying?' for a bit. – But I hope you'll come here in a fortnight.

Love, from us both, to Catherine and you, and little J. P.
D. H. Lawrence

*Wind ?

c/o Mrs Clarke, Grosvenor Rd,
Ripley, Nr Derby.
Friday, 27 Dec., 1918

My dear Katherine, –

We got your parcel on Christmas morning. We had started
off, and were on the brow of the hill, when the postman
loomed round the corner, over the snow. It was all white and
snowy and sunny, with a wind like an axe. I floated out my
hanky for a flag over the snow, and Frieda dropped the tangerines in her anxiety to get the wheatsheaf unwrapped, and it
was terribly cold and windy just on that edge. Frieda's wheatsheaf looked so strange, such a queer indescribable darkish
colour, somehow elephant, over the snow which is so candid
in comparison. It was queer and like Africa, and a bit like a
meteor. She has worn it on her yellow slip, with the red silk
shirt and red coat, at our two parties here – but I can't get used
to it now, it seems like a little torch or brand of elephant-grey,
tropical, lush twilight. Funny how things disturb one. But my
hanky fluttered very nice and lively. I wish you could have
been there on the hill summit – the valley all white and hairy
with trees below us, and grey with rocks – and just around us
on our side the grey stone fences drawn in a network over the
snow, all very clear in the sun. We ate the sweets, and slithered
downhill, very steep and tottering. The children had the
tangerines and the fan.

We read your letter in the wind, dropping down to Cromford. It made me feel weary, that we couldn't be all there, with
rucksacks – I'd got mine on – setting off for somewhere good,
over the snow. It *is* disappointing. And unless one decorates
one's house for oneself alone, best leave it bare, for other
people are all wall-eyed. I do so want to GET OUT – out of
England – really, out of Europe. And I *will* get out. We must
do it.

There was hardly any snow in the valley – all green, with

the yew-berries still sprinkling the causeway. At Ambergate my sister had sent a motor-car for us – so we were at Ripley in time for turkey and Christmas pudding. My God, what masses of food here, turkey, large tongues, long wall of roast loin of pork, pork-pies, sausages, mince-pies, dark cakes covered with almonds, cheese-cakes, lemon-tarts, jellies, endless masses of food, with whisky, gin, port wine, burgundy, muscatel. It seems incredible. We played charades – the old people of 67 playing away harder than the young ones – and lit the Christmas tree, and drank healths, and sang, and roared – Lord above. If only one hadn't all the while a sense that next week would be the same dreariness as before. What a good party we might have had, had we felt really free of the world.

We had a second turn-to yesterday – and at half past eleven went roaring off in the dark wind to Dr Feroze's – he is a Parsee – and drank two more bottles of muscatel, and danced in his big empty room till we were staggered, and quite dazed. Tonight we are going back to Middleton – and I feel infuriated to think of the months ahead, when one waits paralysed for some sort of release. I feel caged, somehow – and I *cannot* find out how to earn enough to keep us – and it maddens me.

Still, it might be very much worse. One might be tied tight to a job, or to a sickness. I do wish you were better. But you *sound* stronger. I long to make *plans* – new plans. But not Europe: oh, God!

I pledge you 'the days to come'.

D. H. L.

60   To Katherine Mansfield

Middleton.
Sunday, 9 *Feb.*, 1919

My Dear Katherine, –
I send you *I Promessi Sposi* and *Peru*. I thought you would like the other two. I am very fond of George Sand – have read

only *François le Champi* and *Maîtres Sonneurs* and *Villemer*. I liked *Maîtres Sonneurs* immensely. Have you any George Sand? And Mary Mann is quite good, I think. It is marvellous weather – brilliant sunshine on the snow, clear as summer, slightly golden sun, distance lit up. But it is immensely cold – everything frozen solid – milk, mustard, everything. Yesterday I went out for a real walk – I've had a cold and been in bed. I climbed with my niece to the bare top of the hills. Wonderful it is to see the footmarks on the snow – beautiful ropes of rabbit prints, trailing away over the brows; heavy hare marks; a fox, so sharp and dainty, going over the wall: birds with two feet that hop; very splendid straight advance of a pheasant; wood-pigeons that are clumsy and move in flocks; splendid little leaping marks of weasels, coming along like a necklace chain of berries; odd little filigree of the field mice; the trail of a mole – it is astonishing what a world of wild creatures one feels round one, on the hills in the snow. From the height it is very beautiful. The upland is naked, white like silver, and moving far into the distance, strange and muscular, with gleams like skin. Only the wind surprises one, invisibly cold; the sun lies bright on a field, like the movement of a sleeper. It is strange how insignificant in all this life seems. Two men, tiny as dots, move from a farm on a snow slope, carrying hay to the beasts. Every moment they seem to melt like insignificant spots of dust; the sheer, living, muscular white of the uplands absorbs everything. Only there is a tiny clump of trees bare on the hill-top – small beeches – writhing like iron in the blue sky. – I wish one could cease to be a human being, and be a demon. *Allzu Menschlich.*

My sister Emily is here, with her little girl – whose birthday it is today. Emily is cooking treacle rolly and cakes, Frieda is making Peggy a pale grey dress, I am advising and interfering. Pamela is lamenting because the eggs in the pantry have all frozen and burst. I have spent half an hour hacking ice out of the water tub – now I am going out. Peggy, with her marvellous red-gold hair in dangling curl-rags, is darting about sorting the coloured wools and cottons – *scène de famille*. It is beautiful to cross the field to the well for drinking water – such pure sun, and Slaley, the tiny village away across, sunny as Italy in its snow. I expect Willie Hopkin will come to-day.

Well – life itself is life – even the magnificent frost-foliage on the window. While we live, let us live.

D. H. L.

Emily's nickname was Pamela, or *Virtue Rewarded*.

61 TO EDWARD MARSH

Chapel Farm Cottage,
Hermitage, Nr Newbury, Berks.
10 *May*, 1919

DEAR EDDIE, –

Your letter has come this morning, with the twenty pounds from Rupert. Queer, to receive money from the dead: as it were out of the dark sky. I have a great belief in the dead – in Rupert dead. He fights with one, I know. That is why I hate the Oliver Lodge spiritualism – hotel bills and collar studs. The passionate dead act within and with us, not like messenger boys and hotel porters. Of the dead who really live, whose presence we know, we hardly care to speak – we know their hush. Isn't it so?

Thank you for thinking of me. Yes, I am happier now the war is fought with the soul, not with filthy guns.

I'll send an inscribed copy of the *New Poems*. Shall I send *Look!* also?

Yrs,
D. H. LAWRENCE

Albergo delle Palme, Lerici,
Golfo della Spezia.
8th November, 1919

Well, I've got so far – travelling now is the devil, if you can't afford a sleeper. The train sits still half the time to hatch out her ideas for the next kilometre – Paris is a nasty city, and the French are not sympathetic to me. I stayed two nights on the way with rich English people — O.B.M. or O.B. some-thing – parvenu, etc. – great luxury – rather nice people, really – but my stomach, my stomach, it has a bad habit of turning a complete somersault when it finds itself in the wrong element, like a dolphin in the air. The old Knight and I had a sincere half-mocking argument, he for security and bank-balance and power, and I for naked liberty. In the end he rested safe on his bank-balance, I in my nakedness; we hated each other – but with respect. But *c'est lui qui mourra.* He is going to die – *moi, non.* He knows that, the impotent old wolf, so he is ready in one half to murder me. I don't want to murder him – merely leave him to his death.

I couldn't get further than this yesterday. O trains! The sea is marvellous – yesterday a blazing, blazing sun, a lapping Mediterranean – *bellezza!* The south! the south! The south! Let me go south – I must go south – why don't we go to the Pacific? Why don't we? Is it only snipe and pop-guns detain us, or something more?

Italy is still gay – does all her weeping in the press – takes her politics with her wine, and enjoys them. Great excitement over the elections – but lively and amused excitement – nothing tragic or serious.

I am going to Florence tomorrow. You can write me c/o Thomas Cook and Son, Via Tornabuoni, Florence – or you can wait for another letter with an address. For your sleepless-ness, *move* – there is nothing like it – but move away from the old trimmings – move away.

The sea is under the window – the sea! My God what wouldn't I give to sail far off on it – south. What wouldn't I give to be off to Nukehera or Numea. *Bello, bello il mare!* the sea! Let us go.

D. H. L.

63   To W. E. and S. A. Hopkin

Palazzo Ferraro,
Capri, Naples.
9 Jan., 1920

My dear Sallie and Willie, –
Today came the hanky and letters from Florence, after so long a time. But we have been straggling about – to Rome, to the wilds among the Apennines south of Rome – then here. The hanky is very lovely with its green sheen through the red: reminds me a good deal of grass going dark under a heavy crimson sunset. The socialist Roumanian from next door, who would please Willie, save that his Italian is of a Roumanian and difficult brand, brought in the post, and with true socialistic communism must at once carefully fold the hanky and try it round his neck, looking very much pleased with himself, and cocking his black eyebrows. But I did not let him appropriate it.

Frieda came down to Florence about a month ago: a bit thinner for her vegetarianism, but very well: had enjoyed Baden-Baden. Everything is very short there – no fat, no milk, practically no meat, no coal. I must have some things sent from England. The French seem really *foul*, and some of these *trials* by the Allies of condemned German war-officials hideously unjust and Inquisitorial. Ah, Lord, the *filthy* world.

Florence was so nice: its genuine culture still creating a certain perfection in the town: Rome was tawdry and so *crowded*, I hated it. In Picinisco we got right into the wilds, where the ass lived on the doorstep and strolled through the hall, and the cock came to crow on the bent-iron washstand: quite a big, fine-looking house, but lo and behold, one great room was a wine-press, another a corn and oil chamber, and as you went upstairs, half the upstairs was open, a beautiful barn full of maize-cobs, very yellow and warm-looking. The kitchen, a vaulted cave, had never been cleaned since the house was built. One ate one's meals on a settle in front of the great chimney, where the pots swung on the hooks and the green wood sputtered. No one dreamed of a table, let alone a tablecloth. One blew up the fire with a long, long ancient iron tube, with a winged foot to stand in the ashes: and this tube was handed from person to person in the process of blowing up a blaze. Hygienics not yet imagined. Add to this, that all around circled the most brilliant snowy mountain-peaks, glittering like hell: that away below, on our oak-scrub hills, the air had a tang of ice, while the wild river with its great white bed of boulders rushed pale and fizzy from the ice: that there was no road to the house, but everything had to be piled on the ass and forded over the river: that the nearest shop was 1½ hours away, the nearest railway 15 miles of terrific mountain road: and that on the Saturday before Christmas it snowed all day long: and you have it.

We fled here. We got on the ship – a little iron tub of a steamer – takes 4 hours to Capri. Of course the sea rose – we got to Capri, where there is no landing stage, in the darkness about 8.0 at night, after 5 hours' wallowing: the sea so high, that when a boat came to take us off it almost hopped on to our deck, and then fell back into an abysmal gulf of darkness, amid yells unparalleled almost even in Italy. In terror, half swamped, it turned for shore, leaving us rolling with a lot of spewing Italians. We had to put back to mainland, and roll at anchor in the shelter of Sorrento till morning, when once more we pushed across to Capri, as the magnificent red dawn came up over the Mediterranean – and like sacks we were hurled into the curvetting boats.

However, here we are, high in this old palace, with two great rooms, three balconies, and a kitchen above, and an enormous flat roof, one of the most wonderful places in the world: Ischia, Naples, Vesuvius slowly smoking to the north –

the wide sea to the west, the great rock of our Monte Solaro in front – rocks and the gulf of Salerno south. Below us, all the tiny jungle of Capri town – it is about as big as Eastwood, just from the church to Princess Street – oh, less than that, very tight and tiny. Below is the piazza, the little square, where all the island life throbs – across the little gulf of the street by the end balcony is the comical whitewashed cathedral.

The island here is about 1½ miles wide, we're on the very neck-steep round ridge of the hill. Altogether Capri is about 4 miles by 2 miles: but really almost mountainous, sheer precipices above us even here. There are heaps of cosmopolitan dwellers – English, American, Russian by the dozen, Dutch, German, Dane – everybody on this tiny spot. Compton Mackenzie has a nice villa here and does the semi-romantic – but I like him, he's a good sort: also we found Mary Cannan, who was Barrie's wife: also Brett Young, a novelist with wife: and lots of other people if we cared to know them. But I prefer the Italians.

Italy is expensive, but works out with the high exchange about equal to England. It is warm – we have had two fires only, just two evenings. We are thinking of starting to bathe now in the sea, which is very beautiful.

There is a real Italian shop behind Mecklenburgh Square, where you can get good, or at least, *real* oil. But I forget the street. If I can get a sound vessel to send it in, I'll send you some from here. I'll see about it.

My dear Willie, I thought Ada had sent those library books back *long ago*. I'll write her.

I *do* wish you could come out here to see us. Couldn't you manage it? It would cost only the *fare*. Thomas Cook and Son, Ludgate Circus, EC4, will do all your passport business, and tell you everything, if you write them. Why not plunge?

Frieda sends her love, with mine.

D. H. L.

Fontana Vecchia,
Taormina (Messina).
7th May, 1920

Had your letter the other day – glad you are well and gay. Fun if you came to Taormina this summer: but August and September are *supposed* to be monstrous hot. But perhaps you like heat. Anyhow, two hotels will be open, Bristol and San Domenico, and they'll give you pension at San Domenico, the swellest place, for 40 francs a day – which is 10/–. The Bristol is only about 26 or 28 francs. We in our Fontana Vecchia are about ten minutes out of town, lovely and cool. We've had some sweltering days already – but our house with its terraces doesn't get too hot: so many green leaves. Most of the foreigners have gone already. The Taorminese are lapsing into a languor and a sloth. I believe Sicily has *always* since Adam been run by a foreign incoming aristocracy: Phoenician, Greek, Arab, Norman, Spanish, Italian. Now it is people in hotels, and such stray fish as me. They, the natives, verily droop and fade out without us, though they hate us when the exchange is too high.

It is very dry here – all the roses out, and drying up, all the grass cut, the earth brown. There is a lot of land, peasant land, to this house. I have just been down in the valley by the cisterns, in a lemon grove that smells very sweet, getting summer nespoli. Nespoli look like apricots, and taste a bit like them – but they're pear-shaped. They're a sort of medlar. Wish you had some, they are delicious, and we've got tree-fulls. The sea is pale and shimmery today, the prickly pears are in yellow blossom.

I've actually finished my new novel, *The Lost Girl:* not morally lost, I assure you. That bee in my bonnet which you mention, and which I presume means sex, buzzes not over-loud. I think *The Lost Girl* is quite passable, from Mudie's point of view. She is being typed in Rome at the moment, which is going to cost me the monstrous figure of 1000 francs. If the exchange goes right down I'm done.

Meanwhile Secker is actually doing *Women in Love* and *The Rainbow*. That is, he is sending *Women in Love* to press at once, so he says – and *The Rainbow* to follow almost immediately, if all goes well. Of course he is rather in a funk, fearing the censor. I wish someone could hold his hand while he gets the thing through. If there's any legal proceeding *I* shall have to pay for it. Lord, the world is a paltry place. The Great War has made cowards of us all, if it was possible.

However, we'll hope for the best, and devil take the hindmost. Let's hope my *Lost Girl* will be *Treasure Trove* to me.

Meanwhile, life at Fontana Vecchia is very easy, indolent, and devil-may-care. Did you ever hear of a Duca di Bronte – Mr Nelson-Hood – descendant of Lord Nelson (Horatio) – whom the Neapolitans made Duca di Bronte because he hanged a few of them? Well, Bronte is just under Etna – and this Mr Nelson-Hood has a place there – his ducal estate. We went to see him – rather wonderful place ... But perhaps you know him.

> Tell me where do Dukedoms lie,
> Or in the head or in the eye –

That's wrong.

> Tell me where are Dukedoms bred,
> Or in the eye or in the head.

If I was Duca di Bronte I'd be tyrant of Sicily. High time there was another Hiero. But, of course, money maketh a man: even if he was a monkey to start with. How are you? Frieda greets you. Salute your husband from me.

D. H. LAWRENCE

Fontana Vecchia,
Taormina, Sicilia.
20 Jan., 1921

DEAR ELEANOR,—

Well, perhaps you'll be glad you haven't come to Sicily. It thunders and lightens for 24 hours, and hailstorms continually, till there is hail-ice thick everywhere, and it is deadly cold and horrid. Meanwhile the almond blossom is almost full out — a sea of blossom, would be, if it weren't shattered.

I should like to talk to you: but feel myself shut up and I can't come unshut just now. I don't like it.

We made a dash to Sardinia — liked the island very much — but it isn't a place to live in. No point in living there. A stray corner of Italy, rather difficult materially to live in.

I have said I will keep this house on another year. But I really don't believe I shall come back for another winter. The south is so lifeless. There's ten times more 'go' in Tuscany.

If I knew how to, I'd really join myself to the revolutionary socialists now. I think the time has come for a real struggle. That's the only thing I care for: the death struggle. I don't care for politics. But I know there *must* and *should* be a deadly revolution very soon, and I would take part in it if I knew how.

Ask R. what book she means — *The Moose*? But that disappeared with Chapel Farm Cottage.

I enclose 10 francs for those stamps. I hope it is enough. Tell me.

Let's hope we meet when something is doing.

                                                    D. H. L.

Villa Alpensee,
Thumersbach, Zell-am-See,
bei Salzburg, Austria.
3 August, 1921

My dear Catherine, –

I have been waiting to see whether I could really stay on here. You know we are with Frieda's younger sister, Johanna, her husband, son and daughter. The villa is on the edge of the lake, we bathe and boat and go excursions into the mountains. The snow isn't far. And the Schreibershofens are really *very* nice with us. And yet, I feel I can't breathe. Everything is free and perfectly easy. And still I feel I can't breathe. Perhaps it is one can't live with people any more – *en ménage.* Anyhow, there it is. Frieda loves it and is quite bitter that I say I want to go away. But there it is – I do.

There is a very nice flat we can have in Florence, for not very much. Only this terrific heat – when is it going to end? But, anyhow, I shall leave here about 12th August. If it keeps so hot I shall stay somewhere near Meran for a while, and perhaps look around and see if I might like to live there. I don't much want to go back to Taormina again. If the weather breaks, and it rains, I shall go to Florence. We should see you there anyway. We'll write more about that.

It is quite beautiful here. There is a very pleasant, largish peasant hotel which you would like: Lohningshof, Thumersbach, Zell-am-See. It is on this side the lake – across from Zell. And you eat *à la carte,* which is much more satisfactory in this part of the world. The ordinary inexpensive hotel here costs 600 krone a day – mounts up to about 700. You can buy almost anything, with enough krone. But the shops are empty – the land financially and commercially just ruined. There is very good white bread – but the food is monotonous. Still, you'd never know you were in a ruined land. The Austrians are as amiable as ever. Travelling is cheap, and quite easy, and the people honest and pleasant. September is a lovely month too, here. But when I have stayed out my month, I feel I shall have to go.

I hope Don didn't mind my asking him to get the passport forms and fill up his part. Frieda's passport is so full, I don't know how she is going to get into Italy. And both the passes expire end of September. We must get new ones in Rome.

I was very glad to hear the book was done: shall be interested to see it. You will probably now get into the real swing for writing.

I shall let you know my movements. We might even meet in Meran or Bozen. That is Italy now, but full Tyrol. It is never *too* hot here – but it must be pretty bad in town.

Au revoir,

D. H. LAWRENCE

67   TO MRS R. P.

R.M.S. 'Osterley.'
Wednesday, 8 *March,* 1922

MY DEAR ROSALIND, –

Here we are on the ship – ten days at sea. It is rather lovely – perfect weather all the time, ship steady as can be, enough wind now to keep it cool. We went on shore at Port Said – and it's still like Arabian Nights, spite of all. Then I loved coming through the Suez Canal – 5 miles an hour – takes 18 hours. You see the desert, the sandhills, the low palm trees, Arabs with camels working at the side. I like it so much. Now we are in the Arabian Sea, and expect to come to Colombo on Monday morning: 15 days' voyage.

The ship is *so* pleasant – only about half full – or less – so plenty of room. We have come second class, and it is perfectly comfortable and nice, couldn't want anything better. Alas, it cost £140 for the two of us. But I had to get out of Europe. In Ceylon we stay with friends. There are children on board having the time of their lives. I am translating Verga's *Mastro don Gesualdo*, to pass the time. By the way I should be so glad if you would some time send me an old Italian novel or book that you have done with – if it is interesting. I should like to go on reading Italian. The people on board are mostly simple Australians. I believe Australia is a good country, full of life and energy. I believe that is the country for you if you had anything specific in mind. If we don't want to go on living in Ceylon I shall go to Australia if we can manage it.

I ordered you *Sea and Sardinia* and *Tortoises*, I hope you will get them – the former from England, Secker, the latter from America, which takes a long time.

Being at sea is so queer – it sort of dissolves for the time being all the connexions with the land, and one feels a bit like a sea-bird must feel. It is my opinion that once beyond the Red Sea one does not feel any more that tension and pressure one suffers from in England – in Europe altogether – even in America, I believe – perhaps worse there. I feel so glad I have come out, but don't know how the money is going to behave. Can't help it.

Write and tell me all that happens – 'Ardnaree', Lake View Estate, Kandy, Ceylon. It seems difficult in this world to get a new *start* – so much easier to make more ends. F. sends many greetings – she is a bit dazed by the sea.

D. H. L.

68   To Lady Cynthia Asquith

R.M.S. 'Orsova',
to Fremantle.
We get there Thursday.
Sunday, 30th April, 1922

Here we are on a ship again – somewhere in a very big blue choppy sea with flying fishes sprinting out of the waves like winged drops, and a Catholic Spanish priest playing Chopin at the piano – very well – and the boat gently rolling.

I didn't like Ceylon – at least I liked looking at it – but not to live in. The East is not for me – the sensuous spiritual voluptuousness, the curious sensitiveness of the naked people, their black bottomless, hopeless eyes – and the heads of elephants and buffaloes poking out of primeval mud – the queer noise of tall metallic palm trees: *ach!* – altogether the tropics have something of the world before the flood – hot dark mud and the life inherent in it: makes me feel rather sick. But wonderful to have known. We saw — at the — a lonely little glum white fish he was sitting up there at the Temple of the Tooth with his chin on his hands gazing blankly down on all the swirl of the East, like a sort of Narcissus waiting to commit black suicide. The Perahera wonderful – midnight – huge elephants, great flares of coconut torches, princes like peg-tops swathed round and round with muslin – and then tom-toms and savage music and devil dances – phase after phase – and that lonely little white fish — up aloft – and the black eyes and black bright sweating bodies of the naked dancers under the torches – and the clanging of great mud-born elephants roaring past – made an enormous impression on me – a glimpse into the world before the Flood. I can't quite get back into history. The soft, moist, elephantine prehistoric has sort of swamped in over my known world – and on one drifts.

But you said, not about India, but about us. No, I am not angry – no more of my tirades – the sea seems so big – and the world of elephants and buffaloes seems such a vast twilight – and by sheer or mere proximity with the dark Singhalese one feels the vastness of the blood stream, so dark and hot and from so far off. What does life in particular matter? Why should one care? One doesn't. Yet I don't believe in Buddha – hate him in fact – his rat-hole temples and his rat-hole religion. Better Jesus.

We are going to Australia – Heaven knows why: because it will be cooler, and the sea is wide. Ceylon steams heat and it isn't so much the heat as the chemical decomposition of one's blood by the ultra-violet rays of the sun. Don't know what we'll do in Australia – don't care. The world of idea may be all alike, but the world of physical feeling is very different – one suffers getting adjusted – but that is part of the adventure. I think Frieda feels like me, a bit dazed and indifferent – reckless – I break my heart over England when I am out here. Those natives are *back* of us – in the living sense *lower* than we are. But they're going to swarm over us and suffocate us. We are, have been for five centuries, the growing tip. Now we're going to fall. But you don't catch me going back on my whiteness and Englishness and myself. <u>English in the teeth of all the world, even</u> in the teeth of England. How England deliberately undermines England. You should see India. Between Lloyd George and Rufus Isaacs, etc., we are done – you asked me a year ago who won the war – we've all lost it. But why should we bother, since it's their own souls folk have lost. It is strange and fascinating to wander like Virgil in the shades.

Don't buy *Sea and Sardinia* because I shall have to pay Martin Secker for it. He must send it you. It will amuse you.

I'm glad the boys are well, and that Herbert Asquith likes reading other people's books. That's better than having to read one's own: and it's much better to be doing something than nothing. I merely translate Giovanni Verga – Sicilian – *Mastro don Gesualdo* and *Novelle Rusticane* – very good – to keep myself occupied. If your husband would like to read them – the translations – tell him to ask Curtis Brown.

F. greets you.

D. H. LAWRENCE

69   To CATHERINE CARSWELL

Thirroul,
South Coast, N.S.W.
22nd June, 1922

MY DEAR CATHERINE, –

Camomile came last week – reached me here – the very day I sent you a copy of the American *Aaron's Rod*. I have read *Camomile*, and find it good: slighter than *Open the Door*, but better made. Myself I like that letter-diary form. And I like it because of its drift: that one simply must stand out against the social world, even if one misses 'life'. Much life they have to offer! Those Indian Civil Servants are the limit: you should have seen them even in Ceylon: conceit and imbecility. No, she was well rid of her empty hero, and all he stands for: tin cans. It was sometimes very amusing, and really wonderfully well written. I can see touches of Don (not John, Juan, nor Giovanni, thank goodness) here and there. I hope it will be a success and that it will flourish without being trodden on.

If you want to know what it is to feel the 'correct' social world fizzle to nothing, you should come to Australia. It *is* a weird place. In the *established* sense, it is socially nil. Happy-go-lucky, don't-you-bother, we're-in-Australia. But also there seems to be no inside life of any sort: just a long lapse and drift. A rather fascinating indifference, a *physical* indifference to what we call soul or spirit. It's really a weird show. The country has an extraordinary hoary, weird attraction. As you get used to it, it seems so *old*, as if it had missed all this Semite-Egyptian-Indo-European vast era of history, and was coal age, the age of great ferns and mosses. It hasn't got a consciousness – just none – too far back. A strange effect it has on one. Often I hate it like poison, then again it fascinates me, and the spell of its indifference gets me. I can't quite explain it: as if one resolved back almost to the plant kingdom, before souls, spirits and minds were grown at all; only quite a live, energetic body with a weird face.

The house is an awfully nice bungalow with one *big* room and 3 small bedrooms, then kitchen and wash-house – and a plot of grass – and a low bushy cliff, hardly more than a bank – and the sand and the sea. The Pacific is a lovely ocean, but my! how boomingly, crashingly noisy as a rule. Today for the first time it only splashes and rushes, instead of exploding and roaring. We bathe by ourselves – and run in and stand under the shower-bath to wash the *very* sea-ey water off. The house costs 30/– a week, and living about as much as England: only meat cheap.

We think of sailing on 10th August via Wellington and Tahiti to San Francisco – land on 4th September. Then go to Taos. Write to me: c/o Mrs Mabel Dodge Sterne, Taos, New Mexico, U.S.A. I am doing a novel here – half done it – funny sort of novel where nothing happens and such a lot of things *should* happen: scene Australia. Frieda loves it here. But Australia would be a lovely country to lose the world in altogether. I'll go round it once more – the world – and if ever I get back here I'll stay. I hope the boy is well, and Don flourishing, and you as happy as possible.

D. H. L.

70   TO CATHERINE CARSWELL

Taos, New Mexico,
U.S.A.
29th September, 1922

MY DEAR CATHERINE, –
Your letter from the 'Tinner's Arms' came last night. I always think Cornwall has a lot to give one. But Zennor sounds too much changed.

Taos, in its way, *is* rather thrilling. We have got a *very* pretty adobe house, with furniture made in the village, and Mexican and Navajo rugs, and some lovely pots. It stands just on the edge of the Indian reservation: a brook behind, with trees: in front, the so-called desert, rather like a moor but covered with whitish-grey sage-brush, flowering yellow now: some 5 miles away the mountains rise. On the north – we face east – Taos mountain, the sacred mt. of the Indians, sits massive on the plain – some 8 miles away. The *pueblo* is towards the foot of the mt., 3 miles off: a big, adobe *pueblo* on each side the brook, like two great heaps of earthen boxes, cubes. There the Indians all live together. They are *pueblos* – these houses were here before the Conquest – very old: and they grow grain and have cattle, on the lands bordering the brook, which they can irrigate. We drive across these 'deserts' – white sage-scrub and dark green pinon scrub on the slopes. On Monday we went up a canyon into the Rockies to a deserted gold mine. The aspens are yellow and lovely. We have a pretty busy time, too. I have already learnt to ride one of these Indian ponies, with a Mexican saddle. Like it so much. We gallop off to the *pueblo* or up to one of the canyons. Frieda is learning too. Last night the young Indians came down to dance in the studio, with two drums: and we all joined in. It is fun: and queer. The Indians are much more remote than Negroes. This week-end is the great dance at the *pueblo*, and the Apaches and Navajos come in wagons and on horseback, and the Mexicans troop to Taos village. Taos village is a Mexican sort of plaza – piazza – with trees and shops and horses tied up. It lies one mile to the south of us: so four miles from the *pueblo*. We see little of Taos itself. There are some American artists, sort of colony: but not much in contact. The days are hot sunshine: noon very hot, especially riding home across the open. Night is cold. In winter it snows, because we are 7,000 feet above sea-level. But as yet one thinks of midsummer. We are about 30 miles from the tiny railway station: but we motored 100 miles from the main line.

Well, I'm afraid it will all sound very fascinating if you are just feeling cooped up in London. I don't want you to feel envious. Perhaps it is necessary for me to try these places, perhaps it is my destiny to know the world. It only excites the outside of me. The inside it leaves more isolated and stoic than ever. That's how it is. It is all a form of running away from oneself and the great problems: all this wild west and the strange Australia. But I try to keep quite clear. One forms not the faintest inward attachment, especially here in America. America lives by a sort of egoistic *will*, shove and be shoved. Well, one can stand up to that too: but one is quite, quite cold inside. No illusion. I will not shove, and I will *not* be shoved. *Sono io!*

In the spring I think I want to come to England. But I feel England has insulted me, and I stomach that feeling badly. *Però, son sempre inglese.* Remember, if you were here you'd only

143

be hardening your heart and stiffening your neck – it is either that or be walked over, in America.

D. H. L.

In my opinion a 'gentle' life with John Patrick and Don, and a gentle faith in life itself, is far better than these women in breeches and riding-boots and sombreros, and money and motor-cars and wild west. It is all inwardly a hard stone and nothingness. Only the desert has a fascination – to ride alone – in the sun in the forever unpossessed country – away from man. That is a great temptation, because one rather hates mankind nowadays. But *pazienza, sempre pazienza!* I am learning Spanish slowly, too.

D. H. L.

71   To J. M. MURRY

Del Monte Ranch, Questa,
New Mexico, U.S.A.
2 Feby, 1923

DEAR JACK, –

I got your note just now, via Kot., about Katherine. Yes, it is something gone out of our lives. We thought of her, I can tell you, at Wellington. Did Ottoline ever send on the card to Katherine I posted from there for her? Yes, I always knew a bond in my heart. Feel a fear where the bond is broken now. Feel as if old moorings were breaking all. What is going to happen to us all? Perhaps it is good for Katherine not to have to see the next phase. We will unite up again when I come to England. It has been a savage enough pilgrimage these last four years. Perhaps K. has taken the only way for her. We keep faith – I always feel death only strengthens that, the faith between those who have it.

Still, it makes me afraid. As if worse were coming. I feel like the Sicilians. They always cry for help from their dead. We shall have to cry to ours: we do cry.

I wrote to you to Adelphi Terrace the day after I got your letter, and asked Seltzer to send you *Fantasia of the Unconscious*. I wanted Katherine to read it.

She'll know, though. The dead don't die. They look on and help.

But in America one feels as if *everything* would die, and that is terrible.

I wish it needn't all have been as it has been: I do wish it.

D. H. L.

Navojou, Sonoru.

5 *October,* 1923

Dear Bynner, –

Here I am wandering slowly and hotly with Götzsche down this west coast. Where F. is I don't know.

This West is much wilder, emptier, more hopeless than Chapala. It makes one feel the door is shut on one. There is a blazing sun, a vast hot sky, big lonely inhuman green hills and mountains, a flat blazing littoral with a few palms, sometimes a dark blue sea which is not quite of this earth – then little towns that seem to be slipping down an abyss – and the door of life shut on it all, only the sun burning, the clouds of birds passing, the zopilotes like flies, the lost lonely palm-trees, the deep dust of the roads, the donkeys moving in a gold dust-cloud. In the mountains, lost, motionless silver mines. Alamos, a once lovely little town, lost, and slipping down the gulf in the mountains, forty miles up the awfullest road I've ever been bruised along. But somehow or other you get there. And more wonderful you get *out* again. There seems a sentence of extinction written over it all. In the middle of the little covered market at Alamos, between the meat and the vegetables, a dead dog lay stretched as if asleep. The meat vendor said to the vegetable man: 'You'd better throw it out.' The veg.-man looked at the dead dog and saw no reason for throwing it out. So no doubt it still lies there. We went also to haciendas – a cattle hacienda: wild, weird, brutal with a devastating brutality. Many of the haciendas are in the hands of Chinese, who run about like vermin down this coast.

So there we are. I think, when we get to Mazatlan, we shall take the boat down to Manzanillo, and so to Guadalajara. It is better there. At least, there is not a dead dog in mid-market.

Write me a line care Dr Purnell – I am a bad correspondent.

Write to F., care Seltzer. She may be in America again by now.

There is a circus, and lions roaring all night.

This town is a busy new adobe nowhere under a flat sun of brass. The old town was washed out in 1915.

I have letters of introduction to people this way, and so see what it's like.

Greet the Spoodle. Tell him to send me a line. Don't take any notice of my intermittency.

D. H. LAWRENCE

73　　　　　　　　　　　　　　　　To Witter Bynner

110, Heath St, Hampstead, N.W.3.
7 December, 1923

Dear Bynner, –

Here I am – London – gloom – yellow air – bad cold – bed – old house – Morris wall-paper – visitors – English voices – tea in old cups – poor D. H. L. perfectly miserable, as if he was in his tomb.

You don't need his advice, so take it: *Never* come to Europe any more.

In a fortnight I intend to go to Paris, then to Spain – and in the early spring I hope to be back on the western continent.

I wish I was in Santa Fé at this moment. As it is, for my sins, and Frieda's, I am in London. I only hope Mexico will stop revoluting.

De profundis,

D. H. L.

74   To Catherine Carswell

Del Monte Ranch, Questa,
New Mexico.

18 *May,* 1924

My dear Catherine, —

We have often spoken of you lately. I wonder what you are doing. We had your letter about your cottage and Don's job. That was mean, to take the job back again. You *do* have bad luck.

Did I tell you Mabel Luhan gave Frieda that little ranch – about 160 acres – up here in the skirts of the mountains? We have been up there the last fortnight working like the devil, with 3 Indians and a Mexican carpenter, building up the 3-room log cabin, which was falling down. We've done all the building, save the chimney – and we've made the adobe bricks for that. I hope in the coming week to finish everything, shingling the roofs of the other cabins too. There are two log cabins, a 3-roomer for us, a 2-roomer Mabel can have when she comes, a little one-roomer for Brett – and a nice log hay-house and corral. We have four horses in the clearing. It is very wild, with the pine-trees coming down the mountain – and the altitude, 8,600 ft, takes a bit of getting used to. But it is also very fine. – Now it is our own, so we can invite you to come. I hope you'll scrape the money together and come for a whole summer, perhaps next year, and try it. Anyway it would make a break, and there is something in looking out on to a new landscape altogether. – I think we shall stay till October, then go down to Mexico, where I must work at my novel. At present I don't write – don't want to – don't care. Things are all far away. I haven't seen a newspaper for two months, and can't bear to think of one. The world is as it is. I am as I am. We don't fit very well. – I never forget that fatal evening at the Café Royal. That is what coming home means to me. Never again, pray the Lord.

We rode down here, Brett and I. Frieda lazy, came in the car. The spring down in the valley is so lovely, the wild plum everywhere white like snow, the cotton-wood trees all tender plumy green, like happy ghosts, and the alfalfa fields a heavy dense green. Such a change, in two weeks. The apple orchards suddenly in bloom. Only the grey desert the same. – Now there is a thunder-storm and I think of my adobes out there at the ranch. We ride back tomorrow. – One doesn't talk any more about being happy – that is child's talk. But I do like having the big, unbroken spaces round me. There is something savage, unbreakable in the spirit of place out here – the Indians drumming and yelling at our camp-fire at evening. – But they'll be wiped out too, I expect – schools and education will finish them. But not before the world falls.

Remember me to Don. Save up – and enjoy your cottage meanwhile.

Yours,
D. H. L.

75   To J. M. Murry

Del Monte Ranch, Questa,
New Mexico.
3 Oct., 1924

DEAR JACK, –

We had your letter. I'm glad you have a good time on the Dorset coast, with Violet. But don't you become the 'mossy stone' – unless, of course, you want to. And perhaps you will find fulfilment in a baby. Myself, I am not for postponing to the next generation – and so *ad infinitum*. Frieda says every woman hopes her BABY will become the Messiah. It takes a man, not a baby. I'm afraid there'll be no more Son Saviours. One was almost too much, in my opinion.

I'm glad you like the Hopi Dance article. All races have one root, once one gets there. Many stems from one root: the stems never to commingle or 'understand' one another. I agree Forster doesn't 'understand' his Hindu. And India is to him just negative: because he doesn't go down to the root to meet it. But the *Passage to India* interested me very much. At least the repudiation of our white bunk, is genuine, sincere, and pretty thorough, it seems to me. Negative, yes. But King Charles *must* have his head off. Homage to the headsman.

We are leaving here next week. There was a flurry of wild snow in the air yesterday, and the nights are icy. But now, at ten o'clock in the morning, to look across the desert at the mountains you'd think June morning was shining. Frieda is washing the porch: Brett is probably stalking a rabbit with a 22-gun: I am looking out of the kitchen door at the far blue mountains, and the gap, the tiny gate that leads down into the canyon and away to Santa Fé. And in ten days' time we shall be going south – to Mexico. The high thin air gets my chest, bronchially. It's *very* good for the lungs, but fierce for tender bronchi.

We shall never 'drop in on one another' again; the ways go wide apart. Sometimes I regret that you didn't take me at what I am, last Christmas: and come here and take a different footing. But apparently you did what was in you: and I what is in me, I do it. As for —, there is just nothing to say. It is absurd, but there it is. The ultimate son of Moses pining for heavy tablets. I believe the old Moses wouldn't have valued the famous tablets if they hadn't been ponderous, and millstones round everybody's neck. It's just Hebraic. And now the tablets are to be *papier mâché*. *Pfui! carito!* it's all bunk: heavy, uninspired bunk. *Che lo sia!* – Kangaroo was never —. Frieda was on the wrong track. And now — is sodden. *Despedida, despedida Eran fuentes de dolores* – .

The country here is very lovely at the moment. Aspens high

on the mountains like a fleece of gold. *Ubi est ille Jason?* The
scrub oak is dark red, and the wild birds are coming down to
the desert. It is time to go south. – Did I tell you my father
died on Sept. 10th, the day before my birthday? – The autumn
always gets me badly, as it breaks into colours. I want to go
south, where there is no autumn, where the cold doesn't
crouch over one like a snow-leopard waiting to pounce. The
heart of the North is dead, and the fingers of cold are corpse
fingers. There is no more hope northwards, and the salt of its
inspiration is the tingling of the viaticum on the tongue.

Sounds as if I was imitating an Ossianic lament.

You can get me in Mexico:
             c/o The British Consulate,
                   Av. Madero 1,
                      Mexico, D.F.
But I want to go south again to Oaxaca, to the Zapotecas
and the Maya. *Quien sabe, si se puede!*

Adios!

D. H. L.

76   To J. M. Murry

Hotel Francia,
Oaxaca,
Mexico.
15 *Novem.,* 1924

Dear Jack, –
   We've been down here a week now – wiggled for two days
on a little railway through the lonely, forbidding country. It's
only 240 miles south of Mexico City, at that. Oaxaca (you
pronounce it Wa-ha-ka) is a little town, about 30,000, in a
wide valley with mountains round, lonely and a bit lost. It's
not far from both coasts, but there's no railway. You can ride
in 4 or 5 days, either to the Pacific or the Atlantic – if you don't
get shot. The country is always unsettled. They've spread such

an absurd sort of socialism everywhere – and these little Zapotec Indians are quite fierce. I called on the Governor of the State, in the Palace. He is an Indian from the hills, but like a little Mexican lawyer: quite nice. Only it's all just crazy. To-morrow he asked me to go out to the opening of a road into the hills. The road isn't begun yet. That's why *we* open it. And during the picnic, of course he may get shot.

It's the chief market today – such a babel and a hubbub of unwashed wild people – heaps of roses and hibiscus flowers, blankets, very nice wild pottery, calves, birds, vegetables, and awful things to eat – including squashed fried locust-beetles. F. and I bought pots and blankets – we shall move into a house next week, and are collecting bits of furniture from various people. It's the house of an Englishman who was born here, and who is a priest in the Cathedral Chapter. Hon. Dorothy Brett will stay on in the hotel – the proprietress is Spanish and very nice.

But everything is so shaky and really so confused. The Indians are queer little savages, and awful agitators pump bits of socialism over them and make everything just a mess. It's really a sort of chaos. And I suppose American intervention will become inevitable. You know, socialism is a dud. It makes just a mush of people: and especially of savages. And 70 per cent of these people are real savages, quite as much as they were 300 years ago. The Spanish-Mexican population just rots on top of the black savage mass. And socialism here is a farce of farces: except very dangerous.

Well, I shall try and finish my *Quetzalcoatl* novel this winter – see what comes of it. The world gives me the gruesomes, the more I see of it. That is, the world of people. This country is so lovely, the sky is perfect, blue and hot every day, and flowers rapidly following flowers. They are cutting the sugar-cane, and hauling it in in the old ox-wagons, slowly. But the grass-slopes are already dry and fawn-coloured, the unven-tured hills are already like an illusion, standing round inhuman.

No mail here yet – let us know how you all are.

D. H. L.

This address is good.

Del Monte Ranch,
Questa, New Mexico.
20 June, 1925

My dear Catherine, –

I was so ill down in Mexico – in Oaxaca – with malaria, 'flu
and tropical fever – I thought I'd never see daylight. So everything slipped. But we got back here about ten weeks ago, and
I am beginning to be myself again. But it was no joke. – As
far as prosperity goes – I have left Seltzer, who hangs, like a
creaking gate, long: and gone to Knopf, who is a better
business man. But of course I still have to live on what is
squeezed out of poor Seltzer.

We've been busy here – brought a stream of water from the
Gallina Canyon – about two miles – to irrigate the field. But
it's so dry, for all that. The water just disappears. We have
a black cow, whom I milk every morning and evening – and
Frieda collects the eggs – about eight a day – from the eleven
hens. Frieda's nephew, Friedel Jaffe, is staying the summer
with us – he helps. We had an Indian and wife to do for us, till
last week: then we sent them away. 'Savages' are a burden. So
a Mexican boy comes up to help: and even him one has to pay
two dollars a day: supposed to be very cheap labour.

Lovely to think of cherry trees in bloom: here the country
is too savage, somehow, for such softness. I get a bit of a
Heimweh for Europe. We shall come in the autumn – D.V. –
and winter somewhere warm.

Who is the other boy you have with you? One of Goldring's
boys? I don't know.

Glad you liked *St Mawr*. In Mexico I finished my Mexican
novel. It's very different. But I think most of it. – Pity you
don't do any writing.

All good wishes from us both to you and the boy and Don.
                                      Yours,
                                        D. H. Lawrence

Villa Bernardo, Spotorno,
Pro. di Genova.

4 Jan., 1926

Dear Jack, –

À la guerre comme à la guerre! Make up your mind to change your ways, and call the baby Benvenuto.

My dear Jack, *it's no good!* All you can do now, sanely, is to leave off. *À la vie comme à la vie.* What a man has got to say is never more than relatively important. To kill yourself like Keats, for what you've got to say, is to mix the eggshell in with the omelette. That's Keats' poems to me. The very excess of beauty is the eggshell between one's teeth.

Carino, basta! Carito, deja, deja, la canzon, cheto! Cheto, choto! Zitto, zitto, zitto! Basta la mossa!

In short, shut up. Throw the *Adelphi* to the devil, throw your own say after it, say good-bye to J. M. M. *Filius Meus, Salvatore di Nessuno se non di se stesso,* and my dear fellow – *give it up!*

As for your humble, he says his say in bits, and pitches it as far from him as he can. And even then it's sometimes a boomerang.

Ach! du lieber Augustin, Augustin, Augustin – I don't care a straw who publishes me and who doesn't, nor where nor how, nor when nor why. I'll contrive, if I can, to get enough money to live on. But I don't take myself seriously, except between 8.0 and 10.0 a.m., and at the stroke of midnight. At other seasons, my say, like any butterfly, may settle where it likes: on the lily of the field or the horsetod in the road: or nowhere. It has departed from me.

My dear chap, people don't want the one-man show of you alone, nor the Punch and Judy show of you and me. Why, oh why, try to ram yourself down people's throats? Offer them a tasty tit-bit, and if they give you five quid, have a drink on it.

No, no! I'm forty, and I want, in a good sense, to enjoy my

life. Saying my say and seeing other people sup it up doesn't amount to a hill o' beans, as far as I go. I want to waste no time over it. That's why I have an agent. I want my own life to live. 'This is my body, keep your hands off!'

Earn a bit of money journalistically, and kick your heels. You've perhaps got J. M. M. on the brain even more seriously than J. C. Don't you remember, we used to talk about having a little ship? The Mediterranean is glittering blue today. Bah, that one should be a mountain of mere words! Heave-O! my boy! get out of it!

D. H. L.

79   To The Hon. Dorothy Brett

Villa Bernardo, Spotorno, Genova.
2 Feb., 1926

Dear Brett, –

I got the whole of *Glad Ghosts* – and have sent it off. But they'll never find a magazine to print it. They wrote that even *Sun* was too 'pagan' for anything but a highbrow 'review': Fools!

You are right. The London group are absolutely no good. Murry wrote asking me to define my position. Cheek! It's soon done with regard to him. *Pour moi vous n'existez pas, mon cher.*

It's beastly weather, cold and rainy and all the almond blossom coming out in the chill. My sister arrives this day week – Tuesday – in Turin. I shall go up there to meet her. She stays two weeks, and I hope we shall get a trip to Florence and Pisa; and I pray heaven the weather may be different.

What are your plans? Ours are very indefinite. I don't feel like going back to America. I love the ranch, but I feel a revulsion from America, from going west. I am even learning a bit of Russian, to go to Russia; though whether that will really come off, I don't know. We might keep this house on till April. But I simply don't know what I shall do. I wish I wanted to go to the ranch again; but I don't, not now. I just don't. The only thing is to wait a bit.

I've left off writing now; I am really awfully sick of writing. But now Frieda is at it, wildly translating the *David* play into German. She's even done it half. I wonder if it would be a great nuisance to you to post me my typewriter. F.'s daughter, Elsa, is a trained typist and knows enough German to type out this MS. from Frieda's rather muddled books. I tried to hire a typewriter in the village, but without success so far. But if you think it's not safe to post mine, or a lot of trouble, don't bother, and we'll try and get one, just for this job, from Savona. F.'s daughter, Elsa, is arriving next week also: but staying in the little Hôtel Ligure while my sister is here.

If we go to Florence, you might have run up for a trip while we are there. But then, if you were going to England later on, it is a waste to come now. And we really might make a trip to Capri in March. It all depends on your plans for returning to the ranch.

I send a couple of snapshots – Rina Secker takes them: they're good, for such a tiny camera, don't you think?

Sorry the Brewsters snubbed your 'Jesus'. Practise the tiger and the cheetah before you do your 'Buddha'. The beasts come first.

Remember me to everybody.

D. H. L.

80   To The Hon. Dorothy Brett

Villa Mirenda, S. Paolo Mosciano,
Scandicci, Florence.
Sat., 15th May, 1926

DEAR BRETT, –

You will be drawing near to America now. I hope the sea has been decent and the landing will be all right: shall be waiting to hear.

We've taken the top half of this old villa out in the country about seven miles from Florence – crowning a little hilltop in the Tuscan style. Since the rent is only 3,000 liras for a year – which is twenty-five pounds – I took the place for a year. Even if we go away, we can always keep it as a *pied à terre* and let friends live in it. It is nice – looking far out over the Arno valley, and very nice country, real country, pine woods, around. I am reading up my Etruscans, and if I get along with them shall go round to Perugia and Volterra, Chiusi, Orvieto, Tarquinia. Meanwhile we can sit still and spend little. There's only one family of foreigners near – Wilkinsons – sort of village-arty people who went round with a puppet show, quite nice, and not at all intrusive. Then the tram is only 1½ miles, at Vingone, and takes us into Florence in ½-hour. This is a region of *no* foreigners. The only thing to do is to sit still and let events work out. I count this as a sort of interval.

I shall wait to hear how you find the ranch and how it treats you. I do hope there'll be somebody nice to go and live there too and help: you *cannot* be there alone. I often dream of the Azul, Aaron and Timsey. They seem to call one back, perhaps even more strongly even than the place. I don't know what is in me, that I simply can't think of coming back to America just now: something in the whole continent that repulses me.

— wrote me, he expects his second baby in a fortnight – it may be here by now. But he is just the same – sort of under-hand. I can't like him.

Earl found your papers – I have them here – I won't send them to the ranch till I know you are there.

We've had horrid weather – then five days' sun – now again grey and trying to rain. I never knew a spring so impotent, as if it couldn't emerge.

Knopf is printing *David* in America, so there should be time for your cover. If you'd like to see them, write to her, Mrs Blanche Knopf, 730, Fifth Avenue.

Things feel a bit dismal, with the strike in England and so on. There's nothing to do but wait a bit, and see if one's spirits will really rouse up and give one a direction.

I still mistrust Earl, in his letter to me, about India.

Remember me to everybody. It seems so far – I don't know why.

D. H. L.

Villa Mirenda, Scandicci, Florence.
Monday, 5 July, 1926

Dear Secker, –

In the hot weather, the days slip by, and one does nothing, and loses count of time. I have never answered your letter about *Sea and Sardinia*. Every time I thought I'd said, it seems to me a good idea to do a 7/6 edition without pictures, and every time I forgot. But I hope you have gone ahead with it. Do you think it's wise to start doing the other books as cheap as 3s. 6d.? But we can talk about that when we come.

In the real summer, I always lose interest in literature and publications. The *cicadas* rattle away all day in the trees, the girls sing, cutting the corn with the sickles, the sheaves of wheat lie all the afternoon like people dead asleep in the heat. *E più non si frega.* I don't work, except at an occasional scrap of an article. I don't feel much like doing a book, of any sort. Why do any more books? There are so many, and such a small demand for what there are. So why add to the burden, and waste one's vitality over it? Because it costs one a lot of blood. Here we can live very modestly, and husband our resources. It is as good as earning money, to have very small expenses. *Dunque* –

And then we're silly enough to go away. We leave next Monday, the 12th, for Baden-Baden (c/o Frau von Richthofen, Ludwig-Wilhelmstift), and I expect we shall spend August in England. A friend is finding us a little flat in Chelsea. So we shall see you and Rina, and I hope we'll have a pleasant time. I want to be back here for September and Vendammia, because

I like it best here. The Tenente still writes occasionally from Porto Maurizio, where he is transferred: rather lachrymose and forlorn. And we had a post card from your *suocera*.

Reggie Turner came out the other day: he says he's doing that book. But I doubt if he'll ever finish it.

My sisters write extremely depressed about the strike. England seems crazy. *Quos vult perdere Deus – !* Well, it's not my fault. But building your life on money is worse than building your house on sand.

Remember us both to Rina.

A rivederci!

D. H. LAWRENCE

c/o Frau von Richthofen,
Ludwig-Wilhelmstift, Baden-Baden.
Thursday, July, 1926

DEAR ROLF GARDINER, –

Your letter today: as usual, like a bluster in the weather. I am holding my hat on.

But do let us meet. We arrive in London on July 30th – and go to a little flat, 25, Rossetti Garden Mansions, Flood St, Chelsea, SW3. We shall use it as a *pied à terre*. Myself, I have promised to spend some time with my sisters on the Lincs. coast – and to go to Scotland – various things.

I believe we are mutually a bit scared. I of weird movements, and you of me. I don't know why. But if you are in London even for a couple of days after the 30th, do come and see us, and we can talk a little, nervously. No, I shall ask you questions like a doctor of a patient he knows nothing about.

But I should like to come to Yorkshire, I should like even to try to dance a sword-dance with iron-stone miners above Whitby. I should love to be connected with something, with some few people, in something. As far as anything *matters*, I have always been very much alone, and regretted it. But I can't belong to clubs, or societies, or Freemasons, or any other damn thing. So if there is, with you, an activity I *can* belong to, I shall thank my stars. But, of course, I shall be wary beyond words, of committing myself.

Everything needs a beginning, though – and I shall be very glad to abandon my rather meaningless isolation, and join in with some few other men, if I can. If only, in the dirty solution of this world, some new little crystal will begin to form.

Yrs,
D. H. LAWRENCE

83   TO ROLF GARDINER

Villa Mirenda, Scandicci, Florence.
3 Decem., 1926

DEAR GARDINER, –

I was glad to get your letter – wondered often about the Baltic meeting – sounds a bit dreary. I think it's hardly worth while trying anything deliberately international – the start at home is so difficult. But the song-tour sounded splendid.

I'm sure you are doing the right thing, with hikes and dances and songs. But somehow it needs a central clue, or it will fizzle away again. There needs a centre of silence, and a heart of darkness – to borrow from Rider Haggard. We'll have to establish some spot on earth, that will be the fissure into the underworld, like the oracle at Delphos, where one can always come to. I will try to do it myself. I will try to come to England and make a place – some quiet house in the country – where one can begin – and from which the hiker, maybe, can branch out. Some place with a big barn and a bit of land – if one has enough money. Don't you think that is what it needs? And then one must set out and learn a deep discipline – and learn dances from all the world, and take whatsoever we can make into our own. And learn music the same; mass music, and canons, and wordless music like the Indians have. And try – keep on trying. It's a thing one has to feel one's way into. And perhaps work a small farm at the same time, to make the living cheap. It's what I want to do. Only I shrink from beginning. It is most difficult to begin. Yet, I feel in my inside, one ought to do it. You are doing the right things, in a skirmishing sort of way. But unless there is a headquarters, there will be no continuing. You yourself will tire. What do you think? If I did come to England to try such a thing, I should depend on you as the organizer of the activities, and the director of activities. About the dances and folk music, you know it all, I know practically nothing. We need only be even two people, to start. I don't believe either in numbers, or haste. But one has to drive one's peg down to the centre of the earth: or one's root: it's the same thing. And there must also be work connected – I mean earning a living – at least earning one's bread.

I'm not coming to England for the *Widowing of Mrs Holroyd*. I begin to hate journeys – I've journeyed enough. Then my health is always risky. You remember the devil's cold I got coming to England in August. I've always had chest-bronchial troubles and pneumonia after-effects – so have to take care.

How well I can see Hucknall Torkard and the miners! Didn't you go into the church to see the tablet, where Byron's heart is buried? My father used to sing in the Newstead Abbey choir, as a boy. But I've gone many times down Hucknall Long Lane to Watnall – and I like Watnall Park – it's a great Sunday morning walk. Some of my happiest days I've spent haymaking in the fields just opposite the S. side of Greasley church – bottom of Watnall Hill – adjoining the vicarage: Miriam's father hired those fields. If you're in those parts again, go to Eastwood, where I was born, and lived for my first 21 years. Go to Walker St – and stand in front of the third house – and look across at Crich on the left, Underwood in front – High Park woods and Annesley on the right: I lived in that house from the age of 6 to 18, and I know that view better than any in the world. Then walk down the fields to the Breach, and in the corner house facing the stile I lived from 1 to 6. And walk up Engine Lane, over the level-crossing at

Moorgreen pit, along till you come to the highway (the Alfreton Rd) – turn to the left, towards Underwood, and go till you come to the lodge gate by the reservoir – go through the gate, and up the drive to the next gate, and continue on the *footpath* just below the drive on the left – on through the wood to Felley Mill (the *White Peacock* farm). When you've crossed the brook, turn to the right through Felley Mill gate, and go up the footpath to Annesley. Or better still, turn to the right, uphill, *before* you descend to the brook, and go on uphill, up the rough deserted pasture – on past Annesley Kennels – long empty – on to Annesley again. That's the country of my heart. From the hills, if you look across at Underwood wood, you'll see a tiny red farm on the edge of the wood. That was Miriam's farm – where I got my first incentive to write. I'll go with you there some day.

I was at my sister's in September, and we drove round – I saw the miners – and pickets – and policemen – it was like a spear through one's heart. I tell you, we'd better buck up and do something for the England to come, for they've pushed the spear through the side of *my* England. If you are in that district, anywhere near Ripley, do go and see my sister, she'd love it. Her husband has a tailor's shop and outlying tailor's trade amongst the colliers. They've 'got on', so have a new house and a motor car. But they're nice.

Mrs W. E. Clarke,
'Torestin',
Gee St,
Ripley (Derby).

Ripley is about 6 miles from Eastwood, by tram-car.

You should do a hike, from Nottingham–Nuttall–Watnall–Moorgreen reservoir–Annesley–Bledworth or Papplewick and across Sherwood Forest, Ollerton, and round perhaps to Newark. And another do., Langley Mill to Ripley, Ripley to Wingfield Manor (one of my favourite ruins), Crich, and then down to Whatstandwell and up again to Alderswasley and so to Bole Hill and Wirksworth and over Via Gellia, or keep on the high ground from Crich and go round Tansley Moor round to Matlock Bridge, or where you like. But it's real

England – the hard pith of England. I'll walk it with you one day.

Tell me what you think of *Mrs Holroyd*, if you see it.

If they give *David* in mid-March, I shall come to England in mid-February. Then I hope to see you properly.

Keep the idea of a *centre* in mind – and look out for a house – not dear, because I don't make much money, but something we might gradually build up.

Yrs,

D. H. LAWRENCE

'Mrs Holroyd' was an aunt of mine – she lived in a tiny cottage just up the line from the railway-crossing at Brinsley, near Eastwood. My father was born in the cottage in the quarry hole just by Brinsley level-crossing. But my uncle built the old cottage over again – all spoilt. There's a nice path goes down by the cottage, and up the fields to Coney Grey farm – then round to Eastwood or Moorgreen, as you like.

84   To Rolf Gardiner

Villa Mirenda, Scandicci,
(Florence)

11 *July*, 1927

DEAR GARDINER, –

Thanks for the camp report. It's amusing – to a novelist, the thing interesting. I don't believe you'll ever get modern Germans free from an acute sense of their nationality – and in contact with foreigners they'll feel political for years to come. They have no self-possession – and they have that naïve feeling that it's somebody else's fault. Apart from that, they *are lustig*, which the English never are. And I think they are capable of mass-movement – which the English aren't, again not the intelligent ones.

But don't forget you yourself want to be too suddenly and

completely a leader – spring ready-armed from the head of Jove. The English will never follow – not even a handful – you see if they do. They'll come for fun, and if it's no fun – *basta!*

But go ahead – here's nothing without trying.

Fra noi e il paradiso c'è l'inferno e poi il purgatorio.

I shall be interested to know what to make of your 'centre', when you've got it. It seems to me the most important – the world sails on towards a debacle – camps and wanderings won't help that – but a little ark somewhere in a quiet place will be valuable. So make it if you can.

I don't think we shall come to England this summer. We want to leave in a fortnight for a place in Carinthia – then Sept. in the Isarthal near München – then a bit in Baden – then back here. So I can't come to the Cheviots. But one day I really should like to come to one of your meetings, somewhere, if I can come as an outsider, not too strenuous. My health is very tiresome lately.

Good luck, then – and *au revoir.*

D. H. LAWRENCE

By the way, is Götzsche a German or a Jew or a Scandinavian or what, by blood?

Your camp sounded just a wee bit like going to prison for two weeks' 'hard'.

85   TO DR TRIGANT BURROW

Villa Mirenda, Scandicci,
Florence
13 *July,* 1927

DEAR TRIGANT BURROW, –

You are the most amusing person that writes to me. It is really funny – resistances – that we are all of us all the while existing by resisting – and that the p.-a. doctor and his patient only come to hugs in order to offer a perfect resistance to mother or father or Mrs Grundy – sublimating one resistance into another resistance – each man his own nonpareil, and spending his life secretly or openly resisting the nonpareil pretensions of all other men – a very true picture of us all, poor dears. All bullies, all being bullied.

What ails me is the absolute frustration of my primeval societal instinct. The hero illusion starts with the individualist illusion, and all resistances ensue. I think societal instinct much deeper than sex instinct – and societal repression much more devasting. There is no repression of the sexual individual comparable to the repression of the societal man in me, by the individual ego, my own and everybody else's. I am weary even of my own individuality, and simply nauseated by other people's. I should very much like to meet somebody who has been through your laboratory, and come societally unrepressed. Is there anybody? If it weren't for money, the peasants here wouldn't be bad. But money is the stake through the bowels of the societal suicide. What a beastly word, *societal!*

This is to say, if you come to Europe, do let me know. I should like to meet you. I love the way you pull the loose legs out of the tripods of the p-a-ytical pythonesses.

Of course, men will *never* agree – can't – in their '*subjective sense perception*'. Subjective sense perceptions are individualistic *ab ovo*. But do tell them to try! What a scrimmage among the mental scientists, and a tearing of mental hair!

Mental science, anyhow, can't exist – any more than the goose can lay the golden egg. But keep 'em at it, pretending.

I think we shall be in Austria – near Villach – for August and in Bavaria – near Munich – for Sept. Are you coming to Europe? – to the p-a-thing in Innsbruck?

Every Jew is a Jehovah, and every Christian is a Jesus, and every scientist is the Logos, and there's never a man about.

I've got bronchials and am in bed for a bit, and furious.

You can convince a man that he lusts after his grandmother – he doesn't mind! – but how are you going to bring him to see that as an individual he's a blown egg!

I'll try and find your paper on the 'Genesis and Meaning of

Homosexuality' – you should have said 'Genesis and Exodus.'
But I've long wanted to know the meaning – and there you
told it in 1917!

D. H. LAWRENCE

Letters to here will follow on when we move.

86

Mirenda.
Monday

DEAR ALDOUS, –

Many thanks for *Proper Studies*. I have read 70 pages, with a
little astonishment that you are so serious and professional.
You are not your grandfather's *Enkel* for nothing – that funny
dry-mindedness and underneath social morality. But you'll say
I'm an introvert, and no fit judge. Though I think to make
people introverts and extraverts is bunk – the words apply,
obviously, to the *direction* of the consciousness or the attention,
and not to anything in the individual essence. You are an
extravert by inheritance far more than *in esse*. You'd have made
a much better introvert, had you been allowed. 'Did she fall or
was she pushed' – Not that I care very much whether people
are intro or extra or anything else, so long as they're a bit
simpatico. But, my dear, don't be dry and formal and exposition
all that – What's the odds! I just read Darwin's *Beagle* again –
he dried himself – and *tant de bruit pour des insectes!* But I like
the book.

We sit here rather vaguely, and I still haven't been to
Florence. It's colder, and we warm up in the evening. Frieda,
inspired by Maria, has launched into puddings: boiled batter
and jam. I do bits of things – darn my underclothes and try to
type out poems – old ones. Reggie and Orioli and Scott-
Moncrieff and a young Acton came *en quatre* – I poured tea,
they poured the rest.

We shall have to be seeing you soon and making plans for Xmas and Cortina: or rather New Year and Cortina. I think we shall go to Florence for Xmas – somewhere where we can eat turkey and be silly – not sit solitary here. Will you be in Florence, too?

I'm reading Beethoven's letters – always in love with somebody when he wasn't really, and wanting contacts when he didn't really – part of the crucifixion into isolate individuality – *poveri noi*.

Love – whatever that is – to all!

D. H. L.

I don't mean I didn't find the 70 pages good – they're very sane and sound and good – only I myself am in a state of despair about the Word either written or spoken seriously. That's why, I suppose, I wrote this, when I wasn't asked – instead of holding my tongue.

87   To Witter Bynner

Villa Mirenda,
Scandicci, Florence.
13 *March,* 1928

Dear Bynner, –

I sniffed the red herring in your last letter a long time: then at last decide it's a live sprat. I mean about *The Plumed Serpent* and 'the hero'. On the whole, I think you're right. The hero is obsolete, and the leader of men is a back number. After all, at the back of the hero is the militant ideal: and the militant ideal, or the ideal militant seems to me also a cold egg. We're sort of sick of all forms of militarism and militantism, and *Miles* is a name no more, for a man. On the whole I agree with you, the leader-cum-follower relationship is a bore. And the new relationship will be some sort of tenderness, sensitive, between men and men and men and women, and not the one up one down, lead on I follow, *ich dien* sort of business. So you see I'm becoming a lamb at last, and you'll even find it hard to take umbrage at me. Do you think?

But still, *in a way*, one has to fight, but not in the O Glory! sort of way. I feel one still has to fight for the phallic reality, as against the non-phallic cerebration unrealities. I suppose the phallic consciousness is part of the whole consciousness which is your aim. To me it's a vital part.

So I wrote my novel, which I want to call *John Thomas and Lady Jane*. But that I have to submerge into a subtitle, and call it *Lady Chatterley's Lover*. But I am printing here in Florence an unexpurgated edition of this tender and phallic novel, far too good for the public. The expurgated will come in the autumn. But this, the full, fine flower with pistil and stamens standing, I hope to have ready by May 15th – 1000 copies, of which 500 for America, at ten dollars a copy. I shall send you a few little order-forms, and *do* please send a few out for me, to the right people. You can reach a lot of the right sort of people in the Universities. I shall mail direct from Florence, as soon as the book is ready: a good book. And why should the red flower have its pistil nipped out, before it is allowed to appear? So I shall trust you in this.

We are in this house till May 6th, then I don't know where. I want to come to New Mexico – perhaps even earn a little money this way to come with.

Tante belle cose!

D. H. LAWRENCE

88   TO A. HUXLEY

Villa Mirenda.
27th March, 1928

DEAR ALDOUS, –
Your letter yesterday – glad you liked the porc. – I got yesterday two copies of *Scrutinies* – the book with my Galsworthy essay in it. Some of 'em hit fairly straight: but Edwin

Muir, real Scotchy, is overpowered by Bennett's gold watch-chain. I'd like to write an essay on Bennett – sort of pig in clover.

Your ideas of the grand perverts is excellent. You might begin with a Roman – and go on to St Francis – Michael Angelo and Leonardo – Goethe or Kant – Jean-Jacques Rousseau or Louis Quatorze. Byron – Baudelaire – Wilde – Proust: they all did the same thing, or tried to: to kick off, or to intellectualize and so utterly falsify the phallic consciousness, which is the basic consciousness, and the thing we mean, in the best sense, by common sense. I think *Wilhelm Meister* is amazing as a book of peculiar immorality, the perversity of intellectualized sex, and the utter incapacity for any *development* of contact with any other human being, which is peculiarly bourgeois and Goethian. Goethe *began* millions of intimacies, and never got beyond the how-do-you-do stage, then fell off into his own boundless ego. He perverted himself into perfection and God-likeness. But do do a book of the grand orthodox perverts. Back of all of them lies ineffable conceit.

Was in Florence yesterday – saw Douglas – looking very old – off in a week's time to Aleppo – or so he says – by Orient Express – do you remember its time-table in Diablerets ? From Aleppo he wants to go to Baalbek – and then, presumably, to rise into heaven. He's terribly at an end of everything.

I haven't got proofs yet of my novel, but they'll begin this week – and say they'll only take about three weeks. The phoenix is printed, very nice. I shall send Maria one. Orioli is very keen. I've got about two thousand liras in orders. Orioli thinks if we got on well with this book, perhaps he can do others, and the author give him a percentage. Not a bad idea. Might be the nucleus of the Authors' Publishing Society of which I spoke, however, to —, so no doubt he'll bombard you. I don't like his letters : sort of bullying tone he takes, with an offended Jewish superiority.

Did you get the order-forms ? Do get private people to send money if you can – so that I can see if I can sell enough without the booksellers, who take a third commission in America, and a quarter in England – and then hold the book back and sell it for double the price. I hate middle-men, and want to eliminate them as far as possible. If I can carry this thing through, it will be a start for all of us unpopular authors. Never let it be said I was a Bennett.

I was reading Aretino's *Ragionamenti* – sometimes amusing, but not *created* enough. I prefer Boccaccio. We had one sunny day, but grey and windy again now – no fun – F.'s daughter here, but leaves tomorrow. The Wilks mere wraiths, having packed up every old rag, pot, pan and whisker with the sanctity of pure idealists cherishing their goods.

Had a cable from Brett asking me to send my pictures to New York for exhibition on May 1st. Too short a notice.

Wish the sun would shine.

Even if we had to go to Switzerland, we could get away early in July, and go to Toulouse or wherever it is.

89 To M. Huxley

Villa Mirenda, Scandicci, Firenze.
Tuesday, 16 April, 1928

DEAR MARIA, –

Quite a while since we heard from you. F. was in Alassio a week with her daughter Barbara – came back last night. Now we're going to begin to pack. I'm winding up my last picture, too, so I can have them shipped to London. I think I shall send them to Dorothy Warren – they might as well be shown. But I shan't sell them. I'm in the middle of the proofs – shall finish them this week – still haven't got a cover-paper – want to find a good *red* – phoenix in black. I send you one specimen with the bird – paper no good. Have a fair number of orders from England – and the first one from America yesterday. So they're beginning. After having the London people trying to pull me down and make me feel in the wrong about *Lady C.* – Curtis Brown's office *en bloc* – Secker – Cape – , I was quite pleased to have Mrs Knopf's letter saying she liked it very much and they want to publish it. Really, people are swine, the way they try to make one feel in the wrong. – *The Forum* sent me letters written by people who read my story, *The Escaped Cock*, that *The Forum* published in February. Really, they're funny – I am an enemy of the human species, have committed the unpardonable sin, etc., etc. – and a story good as gold. And a woman who's been my friend for years told me on Saturday that my pictures were disgusting and unnecessary, and even old-fashioned. Really, I shall have to buy a weapon of some sort. Wish I had the skunk's.

Did you enjoy the trip north? How well I know Lincoln – used to love it. Did you go to the flat dree coast, and Boston and King's Lynn? Or did you go to Southwell and Nottingham?

Roses are out – and iris just fluttering out. Are you feeling chirpy, both of you? We lunch with Lady Colefax at the Waterfields – who have inherited Janet Ross's place – on Monday. *Beati noi!*

D. H. L.

I liked Lady Colefax – she seemed real – but looked as if she feared I might bite!

　　　　　　　　　　To M. and A. Huxley

Kesselmatte, Gsteig b. Gstaad
(Bern).

15 August, 1928

Dear Maria and Aldous, –

Nothing particularly new here. – Last week I was better, and sun-bathed – this week I've got a cold and feel all hot inside. It's a beastly climate really, hot and cold at once. I'm getting sick of it, hope we can leave in first half of September. But my sister is coming with her daughter for a fortnight end of this month. Then when she goes we can go – presumably to Baden-Baden for a bit – and possibly England. I have it in my mind I want to go back to the ranch – but absolutely – in November. Perhaps we might first go and look at some Etruscan things, for a little *giro* – Arezzo, Cortona, Chiusi, Orvieto, Norta, Bieda – places just north of Rome. What do you say? – But I begin to feel I want to go back to New Mexico. I shall never be well any more in Europe – so dead! Nothing to re-act to. I am still unaware of the fate of *Lady Jane* in America – some copies arrived – then we had cables saying 'wait'. So we are waiting. Not that there is any hurry any more; all the English copies having arrived safety. It has been good fun, really, and worth it. Though the money hasn't all come in, by any means. But I feel I've had another whack at 'em – a good satisfactory whack – and it's for them to feel *minchioni*, not me. How they love to make one *minchione*, with their decayed disapproval. But their turn, not mine. How glad I am to have lost certain of my 'friends' through *John Thomas* – like the Israelites who fell dead when the Magic Serpent was erected. May they all fall dead! Pfui!

Aldous, will you please write me out the words of 'I'll give you one – O!' after *four*? I know as far as 'four for the Gospel Writers'. But 5, 6, 7, 8, 9, 10! I don't know.

I had a copy of *Transition*, that Paris magazine – the Amer. number. My God, what a clumsy *olla putrida* James Joyce is! Nothing but old fags and cabbage-stumps of quotations from the Bible and the rest, stewed in the juice of deliberate, journalistic dirty-mindedness – what old and hard-worked staleness, masquerading as the all-new! Gertrude Stein is more amusing – and some of the Americans quite good. But for prize *jejune pap*, take the letters from Frenchmen at the end – the sheer rinsings of baby's napkins. How feeble the Frenchy mind has become!

D. H. L.

Île de Port-Cros,
Var, France.
14 Novem., 1928

Dear David, —

I hardly recognized you as J. D. — and you must be a man
now, instead of a thin little lad with very fair hair. Ugh, what
a gap in time! it makes me feel scared.

Whatever I forget, I shall never forget the Haggs — I loved
it so. I loved to come to you all, it really was a new life began
in me there. The water-pippin by the door — those maiden-
blush roses that Flower would lean over and eat and trip
floundering round. — And stewed figs for tea in winter, and in
August green stewed apples. Do you still have them? Tell your
mother I never forget, no matter where life carries us. — And
does she still blush if somebody comes and finds her in a dirty
white apron? Or doesn't she wear work-aprons any more? Oh,
I'd love to be nineteen again, and coming up through the
Warren and catching the first glimpse of the buildings. Then
I'd sit on the sofa under the window, and we'd crowd round
the little table to tea, in that tiny little kitchen I was so at
home in.

Son' tempi passati, cari miei! quanto cari, non saprete mai! — I
could never tell you in English how much it all meant to me,
how I still feel about it.

If there is anything I can ever do for you, do tell me. — Because whatever else I am, I am somewhere still the same Bert
who rushed with such joy to the Haggs.

                                        Ever,
                                        D. H. Lawrence

The best address is: c/o Curtis Brown, Ltd, 6, Henrietta
Street, Covent Garden, WC2.

Hôtel Beau Rivage,
Bandol, Var.

28 Dec., 1928

Dear Charles Wilson, –

Many thanks for the calendar and the greeting. Here are three scraps of a sort of poetry, which will perhaps do as a 'message'. I've done a book of such poems – really they are *pensées* – which I shall publish later – but you may as well start in with these three bits.

I hope you got your copy of *Lady Chatterley*. It was finally sent from Florence, so if it doesn't arrive it is lost.

I wonder when we shall come to England. I read with shame of the miners' 'Hampers' and the 'Fund'. It's a nice thing to make them live on charity and crumbs of cake, when what they want is manly independence. The whole scheme of things is unjust and rotten, and money is just a disease upon humanity. It's time there was an *enormous* revolution – not to instal soviets, but to give life itself a chance. What's the good of an industrial system piling up rubbish, while nobody lives. We want a revolution not in the name of money or work or any of that, but of life – and let money and work be as casual in human life as they are in a bird's life, damn it all. Oh, it's time the whole thing was changed, absolutely. And the men will have to do it – you've got to smash money and this beastly *possessive* spirit. I get more revolutionary every minute, but for *life's* sake. The dead materialism of Marx socialism and soviets seems to me no better than what we've got. What we want is life and *trust*; men trusting men, and making living a free thing, not a thing to be *earned*. But if men trusted men, we could soon have a new world, and send this one to the devil.

There's more message – perhaps too strong for you. But the beastliness of the show, the *injustice* – just see the rich English down here on the Riviera, *thousands* of them – nauseates me. Men can't stand injustice.

Happy New Year.   D. H. Lawrence

Hôtel Beau Rivage,
Bandol, Var.

21 Jan., 1929

DEAR ENID, —

Glad to hear you are better and enjoying life. Good thing
we sent you none of the books – just heard from Pollinger that
six copies sent him were confiscated, and two Scotland Yard
officials called to inquire. So the brutes are putting their
ridiculous foot down.

The news about the pictures is that they are going to be
reproduced in a book, in colour – expensive – ten guineas a
copy – book to appear in March, and exhibition to take place
at the same time. I suppose this will really come off.

We are still here. Today the Huxleys – Aldous and Maria –
are due to arrive – suppose they'll stay about a week. Then I
really think we'll really leave for Spain. It's been very cold, but
bright – at last it's grey and warmer – rather nice for a change.
Frieda's daughter was here for a while – and another friend.
Frieda was thrilled about vegetable dyes – I suppose she'll be
trying them, when we get a house. How do you make them
fast? Or don't you?

You might call at Lahr's and see if he has any news.

Just a hurried note – affection from both of us, also to
Laurence.

D. H. L.

94   To M. and A. Huxley

Hôtel Principe Alfonso,
Palma de Mallorca.
Ascension Day (May 9th, 1929)

DEAR MARIA AND ALDOUS, —

I had your letter, Maria, but no post card from Cook's,

Barcelona – and not a sound from Aldous – which made me wonder where he was. However, I suppose you are both in London now, though I don't know where, so will send this to Suresnes.

We are still on the island – but changed the hotel. This is very nice, on the edge of the sea, good food but too much of it – ten shillings a day. We are only four people in the place, so have it to ourselves. The weather continues dry, the island parched, the sun hot, the wind often rather chill. The air itself is cold rather than hot – anyhow, cool. The exchange went down to thirty-seven.

Yesterday we motored to Valdemosa, where Chopin was so happy and George Sand hated it. – It was lovely looking out from the monastery, into the dimness of the plain below, and the great loose roses of the monastery gardens so brilliant and spreading themselves out – then inside, the cloisters so white and silent. We picnicked on the north coast high above the sea, mountainous, and the bluest, bluest sea I ever saw – not hard like peacocks and jewels, but soft like blue feathers of the tit – really very lovely – and no people – olives and a few goats – and the big blueness shimmering to far off, north – lovely. Then we went on to Soller, and the smell of orange-blossom so strong and sweet in all the air, one felt like a bee. – Coming back over the mountains we stopped in an old Moorish garden, with round shadowy pools under palm trees, and big bright roses in the sun, and the yellow jasmine had shed so many flowers the ground was brilliant yellow – and nightingales singing powerfully, ringing in the curious stillness. There is a queer stillness where the Moors have been, like ghosts – a bit *morne*, yet lovely for the time – like a pause in life. – It's queer, there is a certain loveliness about the island, yet a certain underneath ugliness, unalive. The people seem to me rather dead, and they are ugly, and they have those nonexistent bodies that English people often have, which I thought was impossible on the Mediterranean. But they say there is a large Jewish admixture. Dead-bodied people with rather ugly faces and a certain staleness. Curious! But it makes one have no desire to live here. The Spaniards, I believe, have refused life so long that life now refuses them, and they are rancid.

I think we shall stay till towards the end of the month – about a fortnight more – then I want if possible to take a steamer to Alicante or Valencia, and do a trip in Spain – Burgos, Granada, Cordoba, Seville, Madrid. I don't expect to *like* it immensely – that is, sympathetically. Yet it interests me.

Then perhaps we'll go to the Lago di Garda or perhaps for a week to Forte, to see if there is a house there. Since I don't think I want at all to stay permanently in Spain, we'd better cast round for a house before the real hot weather sets in.

And I wonder how you are getting on in England, how it all seems to you. Somehow, I don't want to come. The cistus flowers are out among the rocks, pink and white, and yellow sea-poppies by the sea. The world is lovely if one avoids man – so why not avoid him! Why not! Why not! I am tired of humanity.

But I hope you are having a good time, and remember me to everybody and send a line.

D. H. L.

95   To J. M. Murry

Hôtel Principe Alfonso,
Palma de Mallorca, Spain.
20 May, 1929

DEAR JACK, –

Your letter came on here – I had your other one, too, with photographs of the children – felt so distressed about your wife.

But you see, my dear chap, leaving aside all my impatience and 'don't care', I know well that we 'missed it', as you put it. I don't understand you, your workings are beyond me. And you don't get me. You said in your review of my poems: 'this is not life, life is not like that.' And you have the same attitude to the real me. Life is not like that – *ergo*, there is no such animal. Hence my 'don't care'. I am tired of being told there is no such animal, by animals who are merely different. If I am a giraffe, and the ordinary Englishmen who write about me and say they know me are nice well-behaved dogs, there it is, the animals are different. And the me that you say you love is not me, but an idol of your own imagination. Believe me, you don't love me. The animal that I am you instinctively dislike – just as all the Lynds and Squires and Eliots and Goulds instinctively dislike it – and you all say there's no such animal, or if there is there ought not to be – so why not stick to your position? If I am the only man in your life, it is not because I am I, but merely because I provided the speck of dust on which you formed your crystal of an imaginary man. We don't know one another – if you knew *how* little we know one another! And let's not pretend. By pretending a bit, we had some jolly times, in the past. But we all had to pretend a bit – and we could none of us keep it up. Believe me, we belong to different worlds, different ways of consciousness, you and I, and the best we can do is to let one another alone, for ever and ever. We are a dissonance.

My health is a great nuisance, but by no means as bad as all that, and I have no idea of passing out. We want to leave next week for a short tour in Spain – then go north. So don't think of coming to Mallorca. It is no good our meeting – even when we are immortal spirits, we shall dwell in different Hades. Why not accept it. But I do hope your wife is getting better and the children are well and gay.

D. H. L.

96   To Maria Huxley

Florence.
Wed., 10.*vii.*29

You have heard of the catastrophe, of course – 13 pictures seized and in gaol – yours among them – and threatened to be burnt – *auto-da-fé* – you have no luck in that picture. Frieda is staying on in London, don't know how long – had a telegram, nothing else. Arrived with a nasty cold, in bed two days – *miseria* – guess I got it sitting too late on the beach on Friday, as it was all in my legs and lower man – better now – out this evening for the first time. Shall leave Sunday or Monday, I think for Bavaria – not at all hot here, by good luck – more anon.

D. H. L.

97TO M. HUXLEY

Rottach
Sunday, 15th September, 1929

DEAR MARIA, –

Today you are supposed to be starting off for Paris – hope you'll have a nice trip – wonder if it's hot? Poured with rain in the night, but still quite warm, for here: they say, not been so warm for 105 years – why 105 ? We want to leave on Tuesday. I have come to the conclusion that I loathe all mountains, and never want to be among them again. Also I feel as if wild horses would never again drag me over the German frontier. *Never* come – at least, not now. Yet everybody here is extraordinarily nice, and the place quite beautiful – a few years ago I should have loved it. And now, unfortunately, I hate it – for no apparent reason.

We intend to go straight to the South of France – Cassis or Bandol. When I compare how cheerful and well I was there in Bandol, to what I am here, then I decide to go straight back and look for a house, there near Marseilles. I shall send you an address.

I began the cure, with rhythmic doses of arsenic and phosphorus. At the end of a week I was nearly dead (the new man! the animal basis!). So I dropped the drug side of the cure absolutely, and feel much better. But I go on fairly with the porridge and *Rohkost* – raw fruit and vegetables – and I'm sure that's good for me. I feel in better tone already. But in Germany I feel so feeble, and as if I hardly want to live. How I hate it!

I feel I don't want to go to Spain this winter – don't want to make the effort. And at present I'm a bit fed up with travelling: should like a quiet winter, and if I have the energy and initiative, paint.

Dorothy Warren and her husband were due to meet us, and settle up about the pictures, etc. . . . But yesterday I had a wire from Würzburg saying they couldn't possibly come, must go on to Hungary to buy that jade stuff they sell in their Gallery – ugly stuff . . .

That was a horrible affair of Rosc's *prétendant*, poor devil! I must say, your family is unlucky in its men – your sisters. What a mercy the poor wretch is dead! One can't really stand these horrors!

I suppose you've still got your *Pansies*! More muddle. But I've had £300 for it, anyhow – and another £200 due. You'll get a copy in Paris, in time.

Oh, how many liras did you pay for that gramophone? I'd no idea you paid that bill – but if you paid that, I'm sure there were other bits as well. Don't forget to tell me.

I do hope you'll get your *North Sea*. The Warren has it at her house in Maida Vale.

Remember me to Jehanne, and I do hope she's all right.

I wish I was south of the Alps.

Love,

D. H. L.

98

Beau Rivage.
Sunday (? Oct., 1929)

DEAR MARIA, –

We've taken a little house, on the west shore – a sort of bungalow something like yours at Forte, only bigger – six rooms, bath, little central heating plant, hot and cold water –

town supply of water, quite good and apparently abundant – bare garden, good garage – 1000 frs. a month – and really rather lovely position. We expect to move in on Tuesday – *Villa Beau Soleil*. I think it will be nice and easy. There is a *femme de ménage*, Camille, said to be very good. We have it till end of March – can keep it on if we wish. – You think you might come? – But there are no big old stone villas in great gardens, like Italy. One would have to hunt hard in the country to find a bit of a *château* place – it *might* be possible. These villas – modern, are much easier. And does one, after all, *want* a great stone house? Aren't they a weariness? Here, where one is so much out of doors, a small house is so much more convenient – one opens the door on to a *terrasse* or balcony – we've got a big one – and there one has room. It is sunny and still. Already the visitors are nearly every one gone – the village is nearly as last year. But somehow a bit stunned by the mob of town people that have been here – it was a full season. They will come to life in another fortnight or so. The palm trees are recovered, nearly all, and have new green leaves. But the eucalyptus trees, that were so lovely and tressy, are dead, sawn off, they are now monuments of wood. So the place seems paler, and a bit bare, but Frieda says she likes it better. It is a very still afternoon, the sea very still, blue, but autumn slatey blue, and nothing moving at all – men sitting motionless near the dark nets. I'm fond of the place.

Madame, in the hotel, loves us and is almost bitter that we are leaving her. – Max Mohr is here, but not in this hotel, in Les Goëlands. He is rather like a bewildered seal rolling round. The Brewsters, he and she, *may* come. The girl is at school in England. – I am already feeling better, I felt very *low* in Germany. Frieda's foot almost well, but a bit stiff. She bathes now every day, and says it is lovely. I think I shall bathe from the house.

Do they have, in Paris, that new food Bemax, English – the Vitamin B food? Nichols gave me a tin in Mallorca – it's just like bran, but I've an idea it did me good. It costs only 2/6 or so in England – but would be more in Paris. If you happen to be in the sort of shop that would have it, ask them to send me a tin *by post*, to Villa Beau Soleil, will you? And if you happen to put your nose in a likely book-shop, ask if they have a little brochure on *The Olive Tree* and *The Vine*. I want to write essays on various trees, olive, vine, evergreen oak, stone-pine, of the Mediterranean, and should like a bit of technical *Encyclopaedia Britannica* sort of information. But in both cases, don't go out of your way, it doesn't really matter a bit.

I wish Aldous had gone to see Charlie Lahr in London, and got his copy of *Pansies*. Also we talk of making a little magazine, 12 pp., called *The Squib* – which is merely to put crackers under people's chairs. Little sarcastic or lampooning poems, tiny mocking articles, 50 or 100 words, a series of 'mock' reviews – one man wanted to do a tiny 'shorter notice' on the life of M. M., by —— —— that sort of thing – all anonymous, all *noms de plume*. All short, some caricature, drawings – once a month, 12 pp. – 6d. Just squibs to have little darts of revenge and send little shots of ridicule on a few solemn asses: but good-tempered. Rhys Davies and Charles Lahr would edit it, and I think it would be rather fun. It's badly needed. A squib or two at the old women in government. I'm sure, Aldous, you would be A1 at it.

If you decide seriously you would like a house here, we will tell the agent and look. And we might then take a permanency too. It is an easy place. One can sail from Marseilles to anywhere. And one is in the sun. But I daren't for my life persuade you. Only I think the north is death, I really do.

How long do you think to stay in Spain? I am so thankful for the thought of sitting still, quite still, for a winter. I don't even want to go to Toulon. Nowhere.

Enclose £1 for the gramophone – you didn't tell me how much. Regards to Rose and to Jehanne, she will take things too seriously – what does a little religion matter nowadays!

D. H. L.

Beau Soleil,
Bandol.

Wed., Dec., 1929

Dear Aldous and Maria, –

So you are safely back – that's one mercy, anyhow, and we needn't think of you on rainy, windy days and imagine the little red car ploughing on, ploughing on. Ugh! – I feel I don't want to feel any bad weather or see one single ugly or frightening thing just now – and Spain seems full of frightfulness. As for weather, we get mixed – blue and windy just now, turning colder, I think.

No news here. I sent you a copy of *Pansies*, which — brought from London. He does etchings and drawings, and writes on the Apocalypse – I knew him in the past – he is staying at the Beau Rivage for the moment. But he fills me with the same savage despair with the young Englishman – so without fire, without spark, without spunk – so *ineffectual*. What's the good of such people, though they are clever. They think the whole end of living is achieved if they talk, with a drink, rather amusingly and cleverly for an evening. Bores me — somehow so fatuous.

Yesterday Frieda went to Toulon with —, and she bought six snowy-white cups and saucers, and six snowy-white plates – very inexpensive – after having demanded *des tasses de Limoges*. Then she went to the carpet dept – *Dames de France* — floated down on the salesman and demanded *des tapis de Bokhara, s'il vous plaît!* – and bought, of course, a straw mat for 70 frs. But said to Frieda: 'Frieda, *isn't* it rather lovely, *quite* oriental design – and won't — appreciate it – a touch of the East.' – It was Jap, of course. – They want us to look for a house very near them – but for the moment, the sight of their flurries is enough for me. I am thankful for this unredeemedly modern and small Beau Soleil, taken for 6 months and no more, and am thankful to God to escape anything like a per-

manency. 'Better fifty years of Europe than a cycle of Cathay.'
Well, I've had nearly fifty years of Europe, so I should rather
try the cycle of Cathay. – Douglas sent me his *What About
Europe?* – a bit rancid, perhaps, and sometimes fatuous, but on
the whole he's right – Europe is as reesty as he says.

D. H. L.

Ad Astra, Vence.

Friday

Dear Maria, –
    The two parcels came now – very luxurious. Frieda trying
them all – very extravagant of you to send so much. And
Coréine and the Browning book. It's interesting, the Browning, yet somehow humiliating – bourgeois. The bourgeois at
its highest level makes one squirm a bit.
    I am rather worse here – such bad nights, and cough, and
heart, and pain decidedly worse here – and miserable. Seems
to me like *grippe*, but they say not. It's not a good place –
shan't stay long – I'm better in a house – I'm miserable.
    Frieda has Barbey with her – and Ida Rauh. When do you
think of coming?

D. H. L.

This place no good.

MORE ABOUT PENGUINS
AND PELICANS

Penguinews, which appears every month, contains details of all the new books issued by Penguins as they are published. From time to time it is supplemented by *Penguins in Print,* which is our complete list of almost 5,000 titles.

A specimen copy of *Penguinews* will be sent to you free on request. Please write to Dept EP, Penguin Books Ltd, Harmondsworth, Middlesex, for your copy.

In the U.S.A.: For a complete list of books available from Penguins in the United States write to Dept CS, Penguin Books, 625 Madison Avenue, New York, New York 10022.

In Canada: For a complete list of books available from Penguins in Canada write to Penguin Books Canada Limited, 2801 John Street, Markham, Ontario L3R 1B4.

D. H. LAWRENCE

AARON'S ROD

Aaron is a respected member of a mining community, yet his success stifles him. Pinning his faith on his flute-playing, he breaks with his wife, moves south . . . and meets Rawdon Lilly. The extraordinary relationship between these two men – twin poles of Lawrence's own consciousness – is the central span of this important novel.

SONS AND LOVERS

In *Sons and Lovers*, his masterpiece of naturalism, Lawrence wrestled with a serious and intimate emotional problem – his relationship with his mother.

The Morel family, the counterpart of his own, live on the Nottingham coalfield. Mrs Morel is disillusioned with her husband, a coarse-grained and hard-drinking miner, and centres all her expectations on her sons, especially Paul. As Paul Morel grows older, tensions develop in this relationship: and his passions for two other women become involved in a fatal conflict of love and possessiveness.

D. H. LAWRENCE

JOHN THOMAS AND LADY JANE

John Thomas and Lady Jane was one of the titles D. H. Lawrence considered for his most controversial book, *Lady Chatterley's Lover* – 'nice and old-fashioned sounding' he called it.

This is the second version of Lawrence's novel, in many ways quite different from the first and last: both in the personalities of Parkin the gamekeeper (later called Mellors) and Connie Chatterley, and in the development of the love story. In many ways it can justify Lawrence's belief that his novel was, amongst other things, about tenderness.

FANTASIA OF THE UNCONSCIOUS AND PSYCHOANALYSIS AND THE UNCONSCIOUS

In two brilliant exhortatory essays Lawrence set out to redefine the unconscious as 'only another word for life'. Roused by Freud's resurrection of the unconscious, he describes its biological nature, shows how both society and the individual have failed to exploit it, and suggests revolutionary changes in education to accommodate and develop it.

Lawrence's emphasis on the inarticulate side of human nature is a key to the understanding of his novels; his imaginative arguments and supple prose persuade and excite as disturbingly today as they first did fifty years ago.

D. H. LAWRENCE

THE LOST GIRL

Alvina is determined to break away from her father's
failures. Her self-will leads her into a relationship with a
vaudeville actor – and then to Italy.

But the bond linking this lost girl and her lover, sealed in
the murk and grime of a Midlands town, is subjected to
strains of class, temperament and nationality – until Alvina
becomes involved in an intricate and terrible problem of
choice . . .

KANGAROO

Richard and Harriet Somers leave exhausted post-war
Europe for a new and freer world. In Australia they meet
and become involved with Kangaroo, the awesome leader
of a political group called the Diggers. The consequences
are disastrous . . .

In this partly autobiographical novel Lawrence examines
his political position and explores the sources of power in
individuals, in marriage and in society as a whole.

D. H. LAWRENCE

THE RAINBOW

His study of a Midland family of farmers and the tides of passion and conflict within it.

The Brangwens have been established for generations as a yeoman family on the borders of Nottinghamshire, among the coal-mines – a vigorous and strong-willed breed. When Tom Brangwen marries a Polish widow he discovers that love must come to terms with the other forces that go to make up a human personality.

WOMEN IN LOVE

This magnificent novel, which Lawrence himself considered his best, is the story of the lives and emotional conflicts of two sisters.

Gudrun and Ursula, who appeared in *The Rainbow*, live in a Midlands colliery town. Ursula falls in love with Birkin (a self-portrait of Lawrence), and Gudrun has a tragic and demoniac affair with Gerald, the son of the local colliery owner. Those four clash in thought, passion and belief, and the reader is gripped by deeply held convictions about love and modern society.

D. H. LAWRENCE

APOCALYPSE

Apocalypse was Lawrence's last blast against materialism and intellectual modern man. His poetical commentary on the Book of Revelation condemns the envy of the mediocre masses and upholds the instinctive pagan values destroyed by Christianity, science and democracy. Perhaps the breathless interpretation of symbols, beasts and numbers tells us more about Lawrence than about revelation: nevertheless there is power and poignancy in Lawrence's dying plea for the joy of living 'breast to breast with the cosmos'.

GRAHAM GREENE

BRIGHTON ROCK

Set in the pre-war Brighton underworld, this is the story of a teenage gangster, Pinkie, whose ambitions and hatreds are horribly fulfilled . . . until Ida determines to convict him of murder.

THE POWER AND THE GLORY

Too human for heroism, too humble for martyrdom, the little, worldly, Mexican 'whisky priest' is impelled towards his squalid Calvary as much by his own compassion for humanity as by the efforts of his pursuers during an anti-clerical purge.

THE QUIET AMERICAN

A terrifying portrait of innocence at large and a comment on foreign interference in Vietnam.

THE END OF THE AFFAIR

This frank, intense account of a love-affair tells of the strange and callous steps taken by a middle-aged writer to destroy, or perhaps to reclaim, the mistress who had unaccountably left him eighteen months before.

Also published:

TRAVELS WITH MY AUNT

LOSER TAKES ALL

JOURNEY WITHOUT MAPS

IT'S A BATTLEFIELD

THE COMEDIANS

A BURNT-OUT CASE

With biddy.
This book is bought on 7th May 1983 at Swindon, Ocean Terminal